Hello again!
The last day of the holidays

1 New words and phrases

▸ SB, pp. 10–11 | VOCABULARY p. 202

1 We're enjoying the ________________ day of our holidays on the beach.	Wir genießen unseren **letzten** Urlaubstag am Strand.
2 Our ________________ lesson on Monday is English.	Unsere **erste** Stunde am Montag ist Englisch.
3 We're ________________ from our holiday.	Wir sind **zurück** aus dem Urlaub.
4 I don't like sitting ________________ the bus.	Ich sitze nicht gerne **hinten** im Bus.
5 Some computer games are really ________________.	Manche Computerspiele sind wirklich **langweilig**.
6 What do you do when you ________________ ________________?	Was machst du, wenn du **dich langweilst**?

2 Listen carefully!

01

Höre dir die Sätze aufmerksam an und schreibe das fehlende Wort in die Lücke.

1 This is Harry's ________________ week in Spain.

2 Today is the ________________ day of the new school year.

3 Tom and Kim are happy to be ________________ at school.

4 Tom wants to see his ________________ again.

5 Harry thinks the summer holidays are ________________ short.

6 Kim thinks long holidays are ________________.

7 Tom has lots of hobbies, so he's never ________________.

8 Do you like ________________?

Unit 1
Travel and holidays

1 New words and phrases

► SB, pp. 12–13 | VOCABULARY p. 202

1	Last week ____________ in England with my class.	Letzte Woche **war ich** mit meiner Klasse in England.
2	____________ in Brighton and London.	**Wir waren** in Brighton und London.
3	____________ away in the holidays.	**Ich war nicht** weg in den Ferien.
4	____________ at home last week.	**Wir waren** letzte Woche **nicht** zu Hause.
5	You can see Ben Nevis from the ____________ near Fort William.	Man kann Ben Nevis vom **Campingplatz** bei Fort William aus sehen.
6	My family and I were in a holiday ____________ in Brighton.	Meine Familie und ich waren in einer Ferien**wohnung** in Brighton.
7	Molly has a ____________ brother.	Molly hat einen **kleinen** Bruder.

2 New words and phrases

► SB, p. 14 | VOCABULARY p. 203

1	Liz can't ____________ her head.	Liz kann ihren Kopf nicht **bewegen**.
2	She also has a problem with her ____________.	Sie hat auch ein Problem mit ihrem **Fuß**.
3	Don't put your dirty ____________ on the sofa.	Leg deine schmutzigen **Füße** nicht aufs Sofa.
4	There are lots of trees in my ____________.	In meiner **Straße** gibt es viele Bäume.
5	Do you have any ____________ for the weekend?	Hast du **Pläne** für das Wochenende?
6	Let's ____________ a nice present for Mum.	Lass uns **nach** einem schönen Geschenk für Mama **Ausschau halten**.

3 New words and phrases

► SB, p. 15 | VOCABULARY p. 203

1	John goes swimming ____________ day.	John geht **jeden** Tag schwimmen.
2	Can we go ____________ town today?	Können wir heute **in** die Stadt gehen?
3	It started to rain ____________ we were in the park.	Es fing an zu regnen, **als** wir im Park waren.

► Check

4 New words and phrases

▸ SB, p. 16 | VOCABULARY pp. 203–204

1	We ________________ shopping yesterday.	Wir **sind** gestern einkaufen **gegangen**.
2	You can go to Britain by ________________.	Man kann mit dem **Flugzeug** nach Großbritannien reisen.
3	We ________________ lots of funny things with our parents at the weekend.	Wir **haben** viele lustige Sachen mit unseren Eltern am Wochenende **gemacht**.
4	I ________________ elephants in the zoo at the weekend.	Ich **habe** am Wochenende Elefanten im Zoo **gesehen**.
5	I would like to see some ________________ in London.	Ich würde gerne ein paar **Sehenswürdigkeiten** in London sehen.
6	The film is too ________________ for kids.	Der Film ist zu **gruselig** für Kinder.
7	Tom can bark ________________ a dog.	Tom kann **wie** ein Hund bellen.
8	Are you scared of ________________?	Hast du Angst vor **Vampiren**?
9	When Molly was little, her father ________________ her lots of funny stories.	Als Molly klein war, **erzählte** ihr Vater ihr viele lustige Geschichten.
10	The sea was ________________ cold.	Das Meer war **ein bisschen** kalt.
11	Tarek ________________ his homework now.	Tarek **muss** jetzt seine Hausaufgaben **machen**.
12	When her parents weren't at home, Molly ________________ make dinner.	Wenn ihre Eltern nicht zu Hause waren, **musste** Molly Abendbrot machen.
13	I wanted to watch TV, but Mum ________________ "no".	Ich wollte Fernsehen, aber Mama **sagte** „Nein".
14	I ________________ when the big dog barked at me.	Ich **zuckte vor Schreck zusammen**, als mich der große Hund anbellte.
15	Don't ________________ your little brother when he is wrong about something.	**Lach** nicht **über** deinen kleinen Bruder, wenn er etwas falschmacht.
16	The Thames is a big ________________.	Die Themse ist ein großer **Fluss**.
17	Cem's family has a ________________.	Cems Familie hat ein **Restaurant**.
18	Our school ________________ was really great.	Unser Schul**ausflug** war richtig toll.
19	We visited Edinburgh ________________ when we were in Scotland.	Wir haben uns die **Burg** in Edinburgh angesehen, als wir in Schottland waren.

5 What's the word: *was* or *were*?

Vervollständige die Sätze mit den Wörtern aus dem Kasten.

was • Was • wasn't • were • were • Were • weren't

1 Last week my family and I ______________________ on holiday.

2 ______________________ you by the sea?

3 No, we ______________________. We ______________________ in London.

4 ______________________ your grandma with you?

5 Yes, she ____________________, but my grandpa ____________________ with us this time.

6 New words and phrases

▸ SB, p. 17 | VOCABULARY p. 204

1	Do you watch ____________________ on television?	Siehst du dir **Werbespots** im Fernsehen an?
2	Our train ____________________ at half past 6.	Unser Zug **kam** um halb 7 **an**.
3	Our new ____________________ time is 2 p.m.	Unsere neue **Ankunfts**zeit ist 14 Uhr.
4	Liz lives in a ____________________ apartment.	Liz wohnt in einer **modernen** Wohnung.
5	____________________ in the shop was very expensive.	**Alles** in dem Geschäft war sehr teuer.
6	____________________ from the station to the hotel is free.	Die **Beförderung** vom Bahnhof zum Hotel ist kostenlos.

7 Word snake

Finde sechs Wörter in der Schlange und setze sie in die richtigen Lücken ein.

1 Tim went to London by ______________________.

2 He wanted to see the ______________________.

3 How was your class ______________________?

4 Be careful when you go across the ______________________.

5 Molly lives in a small ______________________.

6 She stayed on a ______________________ in our holidays.

▸ Check

8 New words and phrases

▶ SB, p. 18 | VOCABULARY p. 205

1 Mick looked at his son with ________________.	Mick sah seinen Sohn mit **Stolz** an.
2 He was ____________________ of his son.	Er war **stolz** auf seinen Sohn.
3 In the holidays I never ____________________ before 10 o'clock.	In den Ferien **bin** ich nie vor 10 Uhr **aufgestanden**.
4 On school days I get up very ________________.	An Schultagen stehe ich sehr **früh** auf.
5 Please ____________________ me.	Bitte **warte auf** mich.
6 What ______________ does our train go from?	Von welchem **Bahnsteig** fährt unser Zug?

9 New words and phrases

▶ SB, p. 19 | VOCABULARY p. 205

1 A ____________________ ticket is 2.80 €.	Eine **Einzel**fahrkarte kostet 2,80 €.
2 I need a ____________________.	Ich brauche eine **Rückfahrkarte**.
3 England, Scotland, Wales and Northern Ireland are ____________________________________.	England, Schottland, Wales und Nordirland sind **das Vereinigte Königreich**.
4 one ______________, two ________________	ein **Penny**, zwei **Pence**
5 Dogs can't ____________________.	Hunde können nicht **fliegen**.
6 Last year we ____________________ to Spain.	Letztes Jahr **sind** wir nach Spanien **geflogen**.
7 Can we use the pool ____________________?	Können wir den Pool **kostenlos** nutzen?

10 Listen carefully!

02

Höre dir die Sätze aufmerksam an und schreibe das fehlende Wort in die Lücke.

1 Tom and his parents were on a ____________________ in Wales in the summer holidays.
2 Molly and her mum were in a holiday ____________________ in London.
3 Tom's family went swimming ____________________ day.
4 Molly and her mum saw a lot of ____________________ in London.
5 Molly likes stories about ____________________.
6 Eating at a ____________________ in London is often expensive.
7 Tom's family visited two ____________________ in Wales.
8 Tom and Molly enjoyed their holidays and ____________________ a lot with their families.

▶ Check

11 New words and phrases

► SB, pp. 20–21 | VOCABULARY pp. 205–206

1	I ______________ my new shoes to the party.	Ich **habe** meine neuen Schuhe auf der Party **getragen**.
2	I ______________ too much cake at the party.	Ich **habe** zu viel Kuchen auf der Party **gegessen**.
3	I went into town and ______________ a nice present for my friend.	Ich bin in die Stadt gegangen und **habe** ein schönes Geschenk für meinen Freund **gekauft**.
4	Liam collects ______________.	Liam sammelt **Flaggen**.
5	I ______________ a book.	Ich **habe kein** Buch **gekauft**.
6	I ______________ a card for Liam.	Ich **habe** eine Karte für Liam **gemacht**.
7	We need ______________ for the table.	Wir brauchen Tisch**dekoration**.
8	Look, there's a ______________.	Schau mal. Da ist ein **Regenbogen**.
9	I like my brother's new ______________.	Ich mag die neue **Freundin** meines Bruders.
10	My sister doesn't have a ______________.	Meine Schwester hat keinen **Freund**.
11	Are you going to the ______________?	Gehst du zum **Konzert**?
12	Jon's dad is a ______________.	Jons Vater ist **Musiker**.
13	Sorry, I ____________ hear ____________.	Entschuldigung, ich höre **nichts**.

12 New words and phrases

► SB, pp. 22–23 | VOCABULARY pp. 206–207

1	I don't like ______________ toys.	Ich mag kein **Plastik**spielzeug.
2	We need a ______________ of milk.	Wir brauchen eine **Flasche** Milch.
3	When it's cold, I wear ______________.	Wenn es kalt ist, trage ich **Handschuhe**.
4	Marc ______________ an interesting book about seagulls in the library.	Marc **hat** ein interessantes Buch über Möwen in der Bücherei **gefunden**.
5	Tom was in hospital for the first ______________.	Tom war das erste **Mal** im Krankenhaus.
6	______________ I visited my aunt.	**Gestern** habe ich meine Tante besucht.
7	I had a funny dream last ______________.	Ich hatte einen lustigen Traum letzte **Nacht**.
8	Our school trip was very ______________.	Unser Schulausflug war sehr **aufregend**.

► Check

13 Lost words

Vervollständige die Sätze mit den Wörtern aus den Luftballons.

1 I'm looking *for* my sister. Do you know where she is?

2 There's a nice cafe ____________ our street.

3 Don't laugh ____________ your little brother. It's not fair.

4 You can go to Britain ____________ plane.

5 I'd like to go ____________ town at the weekend.

6 I take the bus to school ____________ the morning.

7 Kim has football practice ____________ Friday.

8 It's very quiet here ____________ night.

9 I'm waiting ____________ my friends. They're late.

10 We like sitting ____________ the back of the bus.

11 There were a lot ____________ tourists in London.

12 Our family stayed ____________ a campsite in the summer holidays.

13 There was an ad ____________ minigolf near our campsite.

14 John went to Brighton ____________ train.

14 New words and phrases

▸ SB, p. 24 | VOCABULARY p. 207

1	What ________________ to your arm?	Was ist mit deinem Arm **passiert**?
2	I often ________________ in the sea in the summer holidays.	In den Sommerferien **bin** ich oft im Meer **geschwommen**.
3	How do we ________________ the train station from here?	Wie **kommen** wir von hier **zum** Bahnhof?
4	We ________________ the train in Brighton and ________________ in Southampton.	Wir **sind** in Brighton in den Zug **eingestiegen** und in Southampton **ausgestiegen**.
5	________________ that Tom was your brother. Now I know that he's your cousin.	**Ich dachte**, Tom sei dein Bruder. Jetzt weiß ich, dass er dein Cousin ist.
6	Can I ________________ your cake?	Kann ich deinen Kuchen **probieren**?
7	We watched a ________________ film last week.	Wir haben letzte Woche einen **wunderbaren** Film gesehen.

15 Word partners

Verbinde die Wörter und Ausdrücke, die zusammenpassen.

apartment — wonderful — single — little — next to

small — near — great — flat — one-way

16 Odd word out

Unterstreiche das Wort, das nicht in die Reihe passt.

1 foot – hand – vampire – head
2 plane – car – train – street
3 foot – house – flat – apartment
4 (to) swim – (to) jump – (to) tell – (to) walk
5 (to) tell – (to) eat – (to) say – (to) answer
6 ate – bought – told – fly

17 New words and phrases

▸ SB, pp. 25–26 | VOCABULARY pp. 207–208

1	________ your books on the table, please.	Bitte **legt** eure Bücher auf den Tisch.
2	I can't find my shoes. I don't know where I ________ them.	Ich finde meine Schule nicht. Ich weiß nicht, wo ich sie **hingestellt habe**.
3	Tom always tries to stay ________.	Tom versucht immer, **ruhig** zu bleiben.
4	You ________ too much.	Du **machst dir** zu viele **Sorgen**.
5	Mum ________ always ________ when I come home late.	Mama **ist** immer **beunruhigt**, wenn ich zu spät nach Hause komme.
6	Don't ________ other people's rubbish.	**Heb** nicht den Müll anderer Leute **auf**.
7	Our dog is scared of ________.	Unser Hund fürchtet sich vor **Gewitter**.
8	Can you ________?	Kannst du **reiten**?
9	In the summer holidays I ________ ________ every day.	In den Sommerferien bin ich jeden Tag **auf meinem Pferd geritten**.

▸ Check

18 Lost words

Vervollständige die Sätze mit den Wörtern aus dem Kasten.

bottle • campsite • concerts • musicians • plane • platform • sights • street • thunderstorms • wonderful

1 Tom went to London and looked at the ____________________.

2 Sina's family stayed on a ____________________ in the summer holidays.

3 ____________________ can be scary.

4 Rula and her family went to Spain by ____________________.

5 Liz lives in a quiet ____________________.

6 Tarek had a ____________________ time with his family in Turkey.

7 Molly likes going to ____________________.

8 There are a lot of street ____________________ in London.

9 Our train arrives at ____________________ 9.

10 We need a ____________________ of milk.

19 Different sounds

Welcher Vokallaut klingt anders als die anderen in der Reihe? Unterstreiche das Wort. Suche dann zu jeder Reihe ein passendes Wort im Kasten.

1 bought – all – foot – door ____________________

2 cake – hard – last – laugh ____________________

3 eight – plan – stay – wait ____________________

4 sight – my – trip – write ____________________

5 boat – old – come – no ____________________

6 jump – bus – glove – thought ____________________

come • fast • road • plane • thought • time

20 Opposites

Finde die Gegenteile.

1 late ◄► ____________________

2 boyfriend ◄► ____________________

3 exciting ◄► ____________________

4 first ◄► ____________________

5 single ticket ◄► ____________________

21 Listen carefully!

03

Höre dir die Sätze aufmerksam an und schreibe das fehlende Wort in die Lücke.

1 Our school ______________________ was great.

2 There are some very good ______________________ at our school.

3 Tom needed a ______________________ ticket to London.

4 Trains from Brighton arrive on ______________________ four.

5 Molly ______________________ a wrong ticket.

6 It wasn't easy for her to stay ______________________.

7 She phoned her ______________________.

8 What an ______________________ day!

22 New words and phrases

► SB, p. 28 | VOCABULARY p. 208

1 Swimming in the sea in winter is ______________________.	Im Winter im Meer zu schwimmen ist **verrückt**.
2 A seagull is a ______________________.	Eine Möwe ist ein **Vogel**.
3 Sarah's parents had a ______________________ for her: a trip to Brighton.	Sarahs Eltern hatten eine **Überraschung** für sie: Eine Reise nach Brighton.

23 New words and phrases

► SB, p. 29 | VOCABULARY p. 208

1 Dan and his girlfriend ______________ in town.	Dan und seine Freundin **trafen sich** in der Stadt.

24 What did they do?

Vervollständige die Sätze mit der *simple past*-Form der Verben in Klammern.

1 The Greens ______________________ a nice flat in London. (find)

2 When Sarah was in Brighton, she ______________________ in the sea every day. (swim)

3 The Millers ______________________ a new house last year. (buy)

4 Yesterday we ______________________ at a restaurant. (eat)

5 Lara ______________________ at home in the summer holiday. (be)

6 Tom and Molly ______________________ at the youth centre. (meet)

7 Celia ______________________ to Spain to visit her grandparents. (fly)

8 She ______________________ up very early. (get)

► Check

25 Let's talk: Über Ferienaktivitäten sprechen

▶ SB, p. 197

Ergänze den Dialog so, dass er für dich stimmt. Die Ausdrücke im Kasten können dir dabei helfen. Du kannst deine Antworten auch aufnehmen und jemanden bitten, sie sich anzuhören und dir Feedback zu geben.

I was at home. • Great, thank you. • We stayed with ... • A bit boring. • Yes, we were. • No, we weren't. • I was in ... with ... • We were ...

Hi, how were your holidays? ______________________

What did you do in the holidays? ______________________

____

Were you in a holiday apartment? ______________________

____

26 Let's talk: Über das Wetter sprechen

▶ SB, p. 197

Schreibe die richtigen Sätze oder Fragen aus dem Kasten in die Sprechblasen.

What was the weather like in Spain? • What's the weather like in Britain in winter? • It's often rainy and cold. • It was hot and sunny.

Unit 2
Friends and heroes

1 New words and phrases

▸ SB, pp. 40–41 | VOCABULARY pp. 208–209

Lies die Sätze, sieh dir die Bilder an und trage die richtigen Wörter in das Gitter ein.

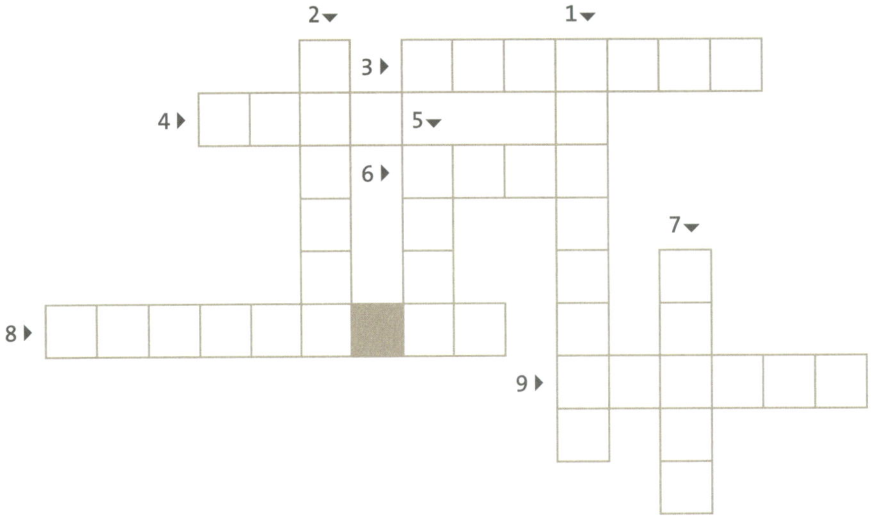

1 The woman has long ??? hair.

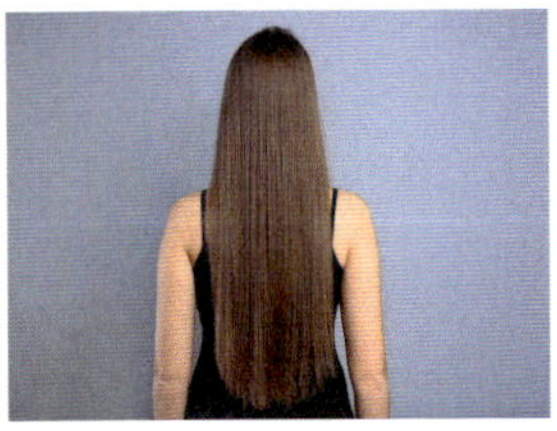

2 The boy is wearing ???.

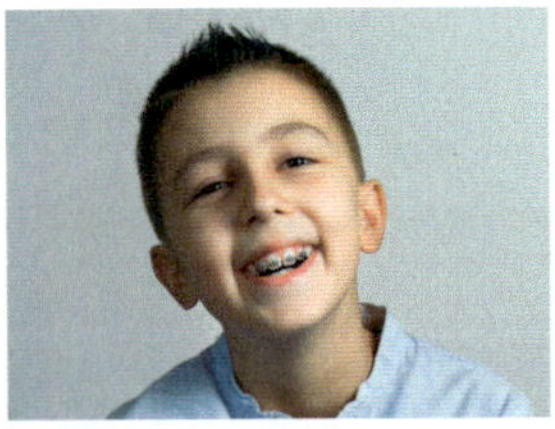

3 The girl is wearing ???.

4 The boy has ??? hair.

5 My brother is my ???. He is always there for me.

6 The boy has short blond ???.

7 The man has ??? hair.

8 Molly often ??? ??? her friends in Germany.

9 Our neighbours are my ??? too. They help everybody in our street.

▸ Check

2 New words and phrases

▸ SB, p. 42 | VOCABULARY p. 209

1	Write a ____________ about your favourite teacher.	Schreibe ein **Profil** über deinen Lieblingslehrer oder deine Lieblingslehrerin.
2	Liam was very quiet when he started school, but now he is a ____________ student.	Liam war sehr still, als er in die Schule kam, aber jetzt ist er ein **selbstsicherer** Schüler.
3	Tom is an ____________ boy.	Tom ist ein **ehrlicher** Junge.
4	Lara and Asif are very ____________.	Lara und Asif sind sehr **mutig**.
5	Can you ____________ your house ____________?	Kannst du **mir** dein Haus **beschreiben**?

3 New words and phrases

▸ SB, pp. 43–44 | VOCABULARY p. 209

1	My dog is very ____________ me.	Mein Hund ist sehr **wichtig für** mich.
2	I ____________ Tom.	Ich **stimme** Tom **zu**.
3	I write with my ____________ hand.	Ich schreibe mit der **rechten** Hand.
4	We share a house with our friends. We live ____________. They live ____________.	Wir teilen ein Haus mit unseren Freunden. Wir wohnen **auf der rechten Seite**. Sie wohnen **auf der linken Seite**.

4 New words and phrases

▸ SB, p. 46 | VOCABULARY p. 210

1	Tom ____________ our cat.	Tom **hat** unsere Katze **gerettet**.
2	Tom, be careful! Don't ____________ into the sea.	Tom, sei vorsichtig! **Fall** nicht ins Meer.
3	The cat wasn't careful and ____________ into the water.	Die Katze war nicht vorsichtig und **fiel** ins Wasser.
4	My name is Alexander, but you can ____________ me Alex.	Mein Name is Alexander, aber du kannst mich Alex **nennen**.
5	Can I ____________ my mum, please?	Darf ich bitte meine Mama **anrufen**?
6	I can't play with you now. I'm waiting for an important ____________.	Ich kann jetzt nicht mit dir spielen. Ich warte auf einen wichtigen **Anruf**.
7	I ____________ my left foot.	Ich **habe** mir den linken Fuß **verletzt**.

5 New words and phrases

► SB, p. 47 | VOCABULARY p. 210

1	Sam wants to ____________ Kim.	Sam möchte Kim **heiraten**.
2	Tom's parents were quite old when they ____________.	Toms Eltern waren ziemlich alt, als sie **geheiratet haben**.
3	John's sister has one ____________, his brother has two ____________.	Johns Schwester hat ein **Kind**, sein Bruder hat zwei **Kinder**.
4	John ____________ in Brighton.	John **ist** in Brighton **geboren**.
5	____________ your dog with me when you go shopping.	**Lass** deinen Hund bei mir, wenn du einkaufen gehst.
6	We ____________ Italy when I was six.	Wir haben Italien **verlassen**, als ich sechs war.
7	Please ____________ me ____________.	Bitte **lass mich in Ruhe**.
8	Sean always liked school. Later he ____________ a teacher.	Sean ging immer gern zur Schule. Später **wurde** er Lehrer.

6 New words and phrases

► SB, p. 48 | VOCABULARY pp. 210–211

1	Lisa is an ____________. She saves animals.	Lisa ist **Aktivistin**. Sie rettet Tiere.
2	Our ____________ is the earth.	Unser **Planet** ist die Erde.
3	Cem works for a ____________.	Cem arbeitet für eine **wohltätige Organisation**.

7 New words and phrases

► SB, p. 49 | VOCABULARY p. 211

1	Cem's house is two ____________ from his school.	Cems Haus liegt zwei **Kilometer** von seiner Schule entfernt.
2	I can ____________ you my phone number.	Ich kann dir meine Telefonnummer **geben**.
3	The dog looked hungry so I ____________ him something to eat.	Der Hund sah hungrig aus, also **gab** ich ihm etwas zu fressen.
4	Molly can't go to school today because she's ____________.	Molly kann heute nicht zur Schule gehen, da sie **krank** ist.
5	Can you do ____________ tricks?	Kannst du **Zauber**tricks?

► Check

8 Listen carefully!

04

Höre dir die Sätze aufmerksam an und schreibe das fehlende Wort in die Lücke.

1 Lucy has long brown ______________________.

2 Liam can't see without his ______________________.

3 Adam has ______________________ on his teeth.

4 I'm ______________________ money for a new bike.

5 Please don't ______________________ the door open.

6 Kerry and Dan got ______________________ in June.

7 It's very ______________________ outside.

8 Lisa's brother has one ______________________, her sister has two ______________________.

9 New words and phrases

▸ SB, p. 50 | VOCABULARY p. 211

1 The wind had so much ________________ that we couldn't walk home.	Der Wind hatte so viel **Kraft**, dass wir nicht zu Fuß nach Hause gehen konnten.
2 This bike costs two ______________ euros.	Dieses Fahrrad kostet zwei **tausend** Euro.

10 Lost words

Füge das richtige Wort aus den Luftballons in die Sätze ein.

1 Describe your house *to* me.

2 Please be careful. The camera is very important ________ me.

3 Tim has an important message ________ Sarah.

4 John always agrees ________ his brother.

5 We have to agree ________ a topic for our presentation.

6 Luca fell ________ the water.

7 Sam's brother was born ________ 2018.

8 Molly shares a room with her sister. Her bed is ________ the left.

9 Sam often thinks ________ his grandpa. He really likes him.

10 Sarah is worried ________ her sister.

11 What happened ________ her?

11 New words and phrases

► SB, p. 51 | VOCABULARY pp. 211–213

1	We can take ______ bus from here.	Wir können **jeden** Bus von hier nehmen.
2	I ______ have ______ questions.	Ich habe **keine** Fragen.
3	Do you have ______ questions?	Hast du **irgendwelche** Fragen?
4	I need new ______.	Ich brauche neue **Stiefel**.
5	Tom wants a ______ bike.	Tom möchte ein **silberfarbenes** Fahrrad.
6	Never cycle without a ______!	Fahr nie ohne **Helm** Rad!
7	Rob would like to swim with ______.	Rob würde gern mit **Delfinen** schwimmen.
8	Mr Cox is a very helpful ______.	Herr Cox ist ein sehr hilfsbereiter **Mann**.
9	Two ______ saved Sarah's horse.	Zwei **Männer** retteten Sarahs Pferd.
10	Don't use ______ near children.	Benutze keine **Chemikalien** in der Nähe von Kindern.
11	Bring your ______.	Bring deinen **Badeanzug** mit.
12	Our planet is the ______.	Unser Planet ist die **Erde**.
13	Horses are ______ animals.	Pferde sind **starke** Tiere.
14	Drawing a ______ isn't easy.	Eine **Nase** zu zeichnen ist nicht leicht.
15	Your ______ are a bit short.	Deine **Hose** ist etwas zu kurz.
16	Most dogs have brown ______.	Die meisten Hunde haben braune **Augen**.
17	I like your vampire ______.	Ich mag deine Vampir**maske**.
18	Let's ______ the tree over there.	Lass uns **auf** den Baum dort **klettern**.
19	Sam's cat doesn't ______ mice.	Sams Katze **tötet** keine Mäuse.
20	Please ______ me.	Bitte **kommen** Sie mit mir **mit**.
21	We ______ home at ten o'clock.	Wir **kamen** um 10 Uhr nach Hause.
22	Mobile phones are very ______.	Mobiltelefone sind sehr **praktisch**.
23	In summer I often wear ______.	Im Sommer trage ich oft **Kleider**.

► Check

12 New words and phrases

▸ SB, p. 52 | VOCABULARY p. 213

1	Sarah had a car ____________________.	Sarah hatte einen Auto**unfall**.
2	There are ____________________ around the park.	Der Park ist von **Mauern** umgeben.
3	Get ____________________ from the tree!	Komm vom Baum **herunter**!
4	John's school is ____________________ the road.	Johns Schule ist die Straße **hinauf**.
5	Our plane ____________________ at six o'clock.	Unser Flugzeug **landete** um sechs Uhr.
6	Lions are ____________________ animals.	Löwen sind **gefährliche** Tiere.

13 New words and phrases

▸ SB, p. 53 | VOCABULARY pp. 213–214

1	It's so dark in here. I can't see your ____________________.	Es ist so dunkel hier drinnen. Ich kann dein **Gesicht** nicht sehen.
2	Sarah's ____________________ hurts.	Sarahs **Knöchel** schmerzt.
3	Please call an ____________________.	Bitte rufe einen **Krankenwagen**.
4	Horses have four ____________________.	Pferde haben vier **Beine**.
5	____________________ me your homework.	**Zeig** mir deine Hausaufgaben.
6	____________________ before you start to sing.	**Atme ein**, bevor du anfängst zu singen.
7	I'm cold. I need another ____________________.	Mir ist kalt. Ich brauche eine weitere **Decke**.
8	I get up early ____________________ I have time for breakfast.	Ich stehe früh auf, **sodass** ich Zeit fürs Frühstück habe.
9	The children were tired and ____________________ ____________________ in the car.	Die Kinder waren müde und **schliefen** im Auto **ein**.
10	Liam ____________________ when his parents came home.	Liam **schlief**, als seine Eltern nach Hause kamen.
11	Liam's uncle likes telling ____________________.	Liams Onkel erzählt gerne **Witze**.

14 New words and phrases

▸ SB, p. 54 | VOCABULARY p. 214

1	Tom ______________ brave when he saved the cat.	Tom **fühlte** sich mutig, als er die Katze rettete.
2	Elephants have a large ____________________.	Elefanten haben einen großen **Körper**.
3	Jack was ill but feels ____________________ again.	Jack war krank, fühlt sich aber wieder **gut**.
4	My phone is ____________________.	Mein Telefon ist **kaputt**.

15 New words and phrases

► SB, p. 56 | VOCABULARY p. 214

	English	Deutsch
1	Let's __________ how we can go to Brighton by train.	Lasst uns **herausfinden**, wie wir mit dem Zug nach Brighton fahren können.
2	How many __________ do you speak?	Wie viele **Sprachen** sprichst du?
3	The English word "brave" is a __________ __________. It looks like the German word "brav", but it means "mutig".	Das englische Wort „brave" ist ein **„falscher Freund"**. Es sieht aus wie das deutsche Wort „brav", bedeutet aber „mutig".

16 New words and phrases

► SB, p. 57 | VOCABULARY pp. 214–215

	English	Deutsch
1	Great Britain is __________ fish and chips.	Großbritannien ist **für** Fisch und Pommes frites **berühmt**. 
2	Mara's cat __________ last year.	Maras Katze **starb** letztes Jahr.
3	Dave __________ the tennis match.	Dave **hat** das Tennismatch **gewonnen**.
4	When Columbus __________ America, he thought he was in India.	Als Kolumbus Amerika **entdeckte**, dachte er, er wäre in Indien.
5	Tom's __________ is British, his __________ is German.	Toms **Mutter** ist Britin, sein **Vater** ist Deutscher.
6	We __________ more trees in our town.	Wir **kämpfen für** mehr Bäume in unserer Stadt.
7	We __________ really hard to win the game.	Wir **haben** hart **gekämpft**, um das Spiel zu gewinnen.
8	Are you for or __________ the new road?	Bist du für oder **gegen** die neue Straße?

17 The fourth word

Ergänze das fehlende Wort.

1 sun – day → moon – __________

2 helmet – head → boots – __________

3 hero – heroes → child – __________

4 up – down → right – __________

► Check

18 Listen carefully!

05

Höre dir die Sätze aufmerksam an und schreibe das fehlende Wort in die Lücke.

1 We had a car ______________ last week, but nobody was hurt.

2 We didn't need an ______________.

3 I need a new ______________.

4 You have to be careful when you work with ______________.

5 These roads are ______________ for children.

6 My cat has green ______________.

7 I'm cold. I need a ______________.

8 Farid speaks four ______________.

19 What's the word?

Vervollständige die Sätze mit den Wörtern aus dem Kasten. Achte dabei auf die Wortart und die richtige Form des Wortes.

~~call~~ • climb • dress • fight • land • laugh • plan • show • surprise • try • worry

1 I wasn't at home when my brother called.

2 I like your blue ______________!

3 Our plane ______________ ten minutes late.

4 Do you have any ______________ for the weekend? We could go swimming together.

5 Molly's friends ______________ her with a chocolate cake for her birthday.

6 I ______________ a really high tree this afternoon. I felt very brave.

7 Do you like quiz ______________?

8 Who started this stupid ______________?

9 Sarah's parents ______________ when Sarah is late.

10 Jim was scared but he ______________ to stay calm.

11 I like my friend because we ______________ a lot together.

20 Different sounds

Welcher Vokallaut klingt anders als die anderen in der Reihe? Unterstreiche das Wort.

1 hair – wear – her – their

2 straight – hard – save – ate

3 first – earth – work – dark

4 learn – here – near – hear

5 by – buy – bye – kill

6 laugh – arm – land – mask

21 What did they do?

Vervollständige die Sätze mit den Verben in Klammern. Verwende das *simple past*.

1 Tom's parents __________ (give) him a bike for his birthday.

2 Mum always wanted to be a teacher, but in the end she __________ (become) a scientist.

3 We __________ (leave) our dog with our neighbours when we went to Italy.

4 Tim __________ (feel) ill, so he didn't go to school.

5 Our team __________ (fight) hard and __________ (win) the game.

8 We waited at the bus stop, but the bus never __________ (come).

22 Let's talk: Sich und andere beschreiben

▸ SB, p. 195

Sieh dir das Bild an und beschreibe die beiden Personen so exakt und ausführlich wie möglich. Die Wörter im Kasten helfen dir. Du kannst deine Beschreibung auch aufnehmen und jemanden bitten, sie sich anzuhören und dir Feedback zu geben.

black • blond • computers • curly • drawing • good at/with • hair • helpful • I think that • kind • (to) look • on the left/right • short • straight • tall

▸ Check

Unit 3
Activities and games

1 New words and phrases

▸ SB, pp. 70–71 | VOCABULARY p. 216

1	Mara likes going to the __________.	Mara geht gern ins **Theater**.
2	The hotel was __________ children.	Das Hotel war **voller** Kinder.
3	This cake is __________.	Dieser Kuchen ist **lecker**.
4	Tom is a very __________ cook.	Tom ist ein sehr **kreativer** Koch.
5	__________ are important animals.	**Insekten** sind wichtige Tiere.
6	Who is your favourite __________?	Wer ist dein/e Lieblings**schauspieler/in**?
7	Do you like __________?	**Spielst** du gerne **Theater**?
8	What'__________ at the cinema this evening?	Was **läuft** heute Abend im Kino?
9	Molly is taking a Spanish __________.	Molly besucht einen Spanisch**kurs**.

2 New words and phrases

▸ SB, p. 72 | VOCABULARY pp. 216–217

1	We often __________ things in our English lessons.	Wir **stellen** oft Dinge **in einem Rollenspiel** im Englischunterricht **dar**.
2	I __________ the guitar every week.	Ich **übe** jede Woche Gitarre.
3	I know I need more __________ to play well.	Ich weiß, dass ich mehr **Übung** benötige, um gut zu spielen.
4	Your toy cat looks very __________.	Deine Spielzeugkatze sieht sehr **echt** aus.
5	Tom's neighbours have a __________.	Toms Nachbarn haben eine **Ziege**.
6	"We'__________ visit our friends in London. What __________ you __________ at the weekend?"	„Wir **haben vor**, unsere Freunde in London zu besuchen. Was **habt** ihr am Wochenende **vor**?"
7	Can you __________?	Kannst du **stricken**?
8	Are you looking for a new hobby? What about __________?	Suchst du ein neues Hobby? Wie wäre es mit **Fotografie**?
9	Students need good reading __________.	Schüler/innen benötigen gute Lese**fähigkeiten**.
10	Molly must __________ the Spanish test next week.	Molly muss sich **auf** den Spanischtest nächste Woche **vorbereiten**.

3 New words and phrases

▸ SB, p. 73 | VOCABULARY p. 217

1 We can ________________ from lots of clubs at my school.	Wir können an meiner Schule zwischen vielen AGs **wählen**.
2 I ________________ knitting last year.	Letztes Jahr habe ich Stricken **gewählt**.
3 My new phone has a good ________________.	Mein neues Handy hat eine gute **Kamera**.

4 New words and phrases

▸ SB, p. 74 | VOCABULARY p. 217

1 On weekdays I get up at ________________.	An Wochentagen stehe ich um **viertel vor 7** auf.
2 I leave the house at ________________.	Ich verlasse das Haus um **viertel nach 7**.
3 On weekdays I come home at ________________.	Wochentags komme ich um **halb 7** nach Hause.

5 Telling the time

Wie lautet jeweils die Uhrzeit auf Englisch? Schreibe sie unter die Zifferblätter.

1

____

2

____

3

____

4

____

5

____

6

____

7

____

8

____

9

____

▸ Check

6 New words and phrases

▸ SB, p. 76 | VOCABULARY p. 217

1 My parents often go to ____________ concerts.	Meine Eltern gehen oft in **klassische** Konzerte.
2 Tim plays ____________ guitar.	Tim spielt **akustische** Gitarre.
3 Ms Brown is ____________ all the students.	Frau Brown ist **bei** allen Schülerinnen und Schülern **beliebt**.
4 Tom is older ____________ Tarek.	Tom ist älter **als** Tarek.

06

7 Listen carefully!

Höre dir die Sätze aufmerksam an und schreibe das fehlende Wort in die Lücke.

1 Sam must ____________ for the Spanish test.
2 Cem's favourite hobby is ____________.
3 He bought a new ____________ online.
4 Tyler wants to become an ____________.
5 Tyler and his parents often go to the ____________.
6 Molly makes ____________ desserts.
7 Students can ____________ from lots of different clubs at Molly's school.
8 Molly ____________ a cooking course.

8 Lost words

Vervollständige die Sätze mit den Wörtern aus den Luftballons.

1 We booked a holiday apartment ___*in*___ Brighton.
2 What's ________ at the cinema ________ the moment?
3 London is very popular ________ tourists.
4 I want to prepare ________ the English test ________ Monday.
5 Can we meet ________ half ________ five?
6 The photography course starts at quarter ________ six.
7 The theatre was full ________ young people.
8 I went ________ Italy last summer.
9 What are you going ________ do at the weekend?
10 Italy is famous ________ good ice cream.

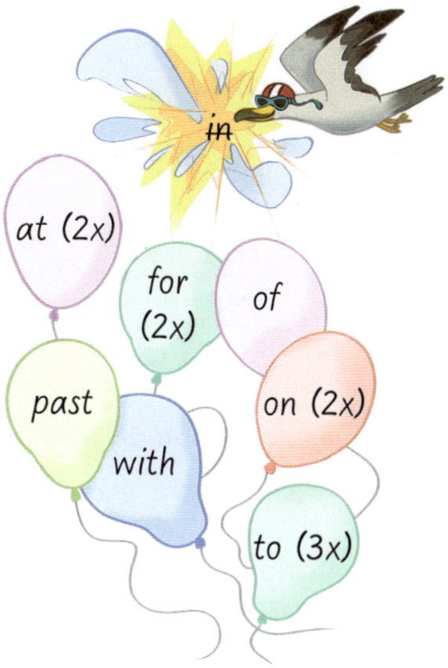

9 New words and phrases

▶ SB, p. 77 | VOCABULARY pp. 217–218

1	Toni's pizzas are good, but not ____________ ________________ Toto's.	Tonis Pizzas sind gut, aber nicht **so gut wie** Totos.
2	The weather was already bad when we arrived and then got ________________ every day.	Das Wetter war schon schlecht, als wir ankamen, und wurde dann jeden Tag **schlechter**.
3	Doing sport is ________________ than watching TV.	Sport treiben ist **besser** als fernsehen.
4	What do you ____________________: cheese or meat?	Was **magst** du **lieber**: Käse oder Fleisch?
5	Classical music can be very ______________.	Klassische Musik kann sehr **entspannend** sein.
6	Tarek is a very ________________ boy. He has lots of ________________.	Tarek ist ein sehr **aktiver** Junge. Er hat viel **Energie**.

10 New words and phrases

▶ SB, pp. 78–79 | VOCABULARY p. 218

1	What was your ________________ meal ever?	Was war das **schlimmste** Essen, das du jemals gegessen hast?
2	And what was your ______________ meal?	Und was war dein **bestes** Essen?
3	Tim's brother is a ______________ and his sister wants to become a ____________ too.	Tims Bruder ist **Arzt** und seine Schwester möchte auch **Ärztin** werden.
4	Molly was ______________________ yesterday.	Molly war gestern **beim Arzt**.
5	Who plays ____________ Cox in the film?	Wer spielt **Agent** Cox in dem Film?
6	All my bookshelves are full. I have no ________________ for books any more.	Alle meine Bücherregale sind voll. Ich habe keinen **Platz** mehr für Bücher.
7	The main ________________ in the film is a little boy.	Die Haupt**figur** in dem Film ist ein kleiner Junge.
8	The summer concerts always ____________ ________________ in June.	Die Sommerkonzerte **finden** immer im Juni **statt**.
9	Tom's party ________________ in May.	Toms Party **fand** im Mai **statt**.

▶ Check

11 What's the word?

Vervollständige die Sätze mit den Wörtern aus dem Kasten.

choose • chose • creates • creative • full of • goats • prepare • preparation

1 My shoes are ______________________ water.

2 Lara ______________________ her own clothes.

3 Can you ______________________ dinner now, please?

4 You can ______________________: chips or potatoes?

5 Tarek is very ______________________. He draws pictures and writes stories.

6 You don't need much ______________________ time for this dish.

7 Farid ______________________ French as a third language.

8 Our neighbours have three ______________________.

12 New words and phrases

► SB, p. 80 | VOCABULARY pp. 218–219

1 A trip to another country is a great ______________.	Eine Reise in ein anderes Land ist ein tolles **Abenteuer**.
2 There's a ______________ over the river.	Es gibt eine **Brücke** über den Fluss.
3 We often go walking in a ______________ near our village.	Wir gehen oft in einem **Wald** in der Nähe unseres Dorfes spazieren.
4 Ben Nevis is a high ______________ in Scotland.	Ben Nevis ist ein hoher **Berg** in Schottland.
5 Tom lives on the third floor and has to climb lots of ______________ every day.	Tom wohnt im dritten Stock und muss täglich viele **Treppen** steigen.
6 I can't find my ______________.	Ich finde meinen **Schlüssel** nicht.
7 Let's walk home ______________ the park.	Lass uns **durch** den Park nach Hause gehen.
8 ______________ at the book shop. Walk to the cinema and ______________ there.	**Bieg** am Buchladen **rechts ab**. Geh bis zum Kino und bieg dort **links ab**.
9 Walk ______________ to get to the school.	Geh **geradeaus weiter**, um zur Schule zu gelangen.
10 Walk ______________ theatre and then turn right.	Geh **am** Theater **vorbei** und bieg dann rechts ab.
11 Let's walk ______________ the bridge.	Lass uns **über** die Brücke gehen.

13 New words and phrases

▸ SB, p. 81 | VOCABULARY p. 219

1	Sina is a very good tennis player. She has lots of ____________________.	Sina ist eine sehr gute Tennisspielerin. Sie besitzt viele **Pokale**.
2	We live on the top floor. There is nobody ____________________ us.	Wir wohnen im obersten Stockwerk. **Über** uns ist niemand.
3	Read the text ____________________.	Lies den Text **oben**.
4	You can sit ________________ Jane and John.	Du kannst **zwischen** Jane und John sitzen.
5	There's a big ____________________ table in our dining area.	Wir haben einen großen **runden** Tisch in unserer Essecke.
6	"I'd like two of these cakes." – "I'm sorry, this is ____________________."	„Ich möchte zwei von diesen Kuchen." – „Tut mir leid, das ist **der letzte**."
7	Lara has two dogs, a ____________________ and a ____________________.	Lara hat zwei Hunde, einen **großen** und einen **kleinen**.
8	What's the _______________ at the moment?	Wie ist der **Spielstand** gerade?
9	The station is at the ____________________ of the street.	Der Bahnhof ist am **unteren Ende** der Straße.
10	Tom is proud when he gets to the next ___________________ in his computer game.	Tom ist stolz, wenn er das nächste **Level** in seinem Computerspiel erreicht.

14 What's the word: *one* or *ones*?

Vervollständige die Sätze mit den richtigen Wörtern.

1 "I like the T-shirt." – "Which _______________? The red _______________ or the green _______________?" – "The green _______________."

2 Mario has four cats, two brown _______________ and two black _______________. One of the black _______________ is quite old.

3 Luke needs some new trousers. His old _______________ are too small.

▸ Check

lighthouse 2

BASIC

Wordmaster

Lösungen

Cornelsen

Hello again! The last days of the holidays

1 New words and phrases
► SB, pp. 10-11 | VOCABULARY p. 202

1 last • **2** first • **3** back • **4** at the back of • **5** boring • **6** 're/are/get bored

2 Listen carefully!

1 last • **2** first • **3** back • **4** friends • **5** too • **6** boring • **7** bored • **8** ice cream

Unit 1: Travel and holidays

1 New words and phrases
► SB, pp. 12–13 | VOCABULARY p. 202

1 I was • **2** We were • **3** I wasn't / I was not • **4** We weren't / We were not • **5** campsite • **6** apartment/flat • **7** little

2 New words and phrases
► SB, p. 14 | VOCABULARY p. 203

1 move • **2** foot • **3** feet • **4** street • **5** plans • **6** look for

3 New words and phrases
► SB, p. 15 | VOCABULARY p. 203

1 every • **2** into • **3** when

4 New words and phrases
► SB, p. 16 | VOCABULARY pp. 203–204

1 went • **2** plane • **3** did • **4** saw • **5** sights • **6** scary • **7** like • **8** vampires • **9** told • **10** a bit • **11** has to do • **12** had to • **13** said • **14** jumped • **15** laugh at • **16** river • **17** restaurant • **18** trip • **19** Castle

5 What's the word: *was* or *were*?

1 were • **2** Were • **3** weren't; were • **4** Was • **5** was; wasn't

6 New words and phrases
► SB, p. 17 | VOCABULARY p. 204

1 adverts/ads • **2** arrived • **3** arrival • **4** modern • **5** Everything • **6** Transport

7 Word snake

1 plane • **2** sights • **3** trip • **4** street • **5** apartment • **6** campsite

8 New words and phrases
► SB, p. 18 | VOCABULARY p. 205

1 pride • **2** proud • **3** got up • **4** early • **5** wait for • **6** platform

9 New words and phrases
► SB, p. 19 | VOCABULARY p. 205

1 single / one-way ticket • **2** return (ticket) • **3** the United Kingdom / the UK • **4** penny; pence • **5** fly • **6** flew • **7** for free

10 Listen carefully!

1 campsite • **2** apartment • **3** every • **4** sights • **5** vampires • **6** restaurant • **7** castles • **8** laughed

11 New words and phrases

▸ SB, pp. 20–21 | VOCABULARY pp. 205–206

1 wore • **2** ate • **3** bought • **4** flags • **5** didn't buy / did not buy • **6** made • **7** decoration • **8** rainbow • **9** girlfriend • **10** boyfriend • **11** concert • **12** musician • **13** don't; anything

12 New words and phrases

▸ SB, pp. 22–23 | VOCABULARY pp. 206–207

1 plastic • **2** bottle • **3** gloves • **4** found • **5** time • **6** Yesterday • **7** night • **8** exciting

13 Lost words

1 for • **2** on • **3** at • **4** by • **5** into • **6** in • **7** on • **8** at • **9** for • **10** at • **11** of • **12** on • **13** for • **14** by

14 New words and phrases

▸ SB, p. 24 | VOCABULARY p. 207

1 happened • **2** swam • **3** get to • **4** got on; got off • **5** I thought • **6** try • **7** wonderful

15 Word partners

1 apartment – flat • **2** wonderful – great • **3** single – one-way • **4** little – small • **5** next to – near

16 Odd word out

1 vampire • **2** street • **3** foot • **4** (to) tell • **5** (to) eat • **6** fly

17 New words and phrases

▸ SB, pp. 25–26 | VOCABULARY pp. 207–208

1 Put • **2** put • **3** calm • **4** worry • **5** Is; worried • **6** pick up • **7** thunderstorms • **8** ride a horse • **9** rode my horse

18 Lost words

1 sights • **2** campsite • **3** Thunderstorms • **4** plane • **5** street • **6** wonderful • **7** concerts • **8** musicians • **9** platform • **10** bottle

19 Different sounds

1 <u>foot</u>; thought • **2** <u>cake</u>; fast • **3** <u>plan</u>; plane • **4** <u>trip</u>; time • **5** <u>come</u>; road • **6** <u>thought</u>; come

20 Opposites

1 early • **2** girlfriend • **3** boring • **4** last • **7** return ticket

21 Listen carefully!

1 concert • **2** musicians • **3** return • **4** platform • **5** bought • **6** calm • **7** boyfriend • **8** exciting

22 New words and phrases

▸ SB, p. 28 | VOCABULARY p. 208

1 crazy • **2** bird • **3** surprise

23 New words and phrases

▸ SB, p. 29 | VOCABULARY p. 208

1 met

24 What did they do?

1 found • **2** swam • **3** bought • **4** ate • **5** was • **6** met • **7** flew • **8** got

25 Let's talk: Über Ferienaktivitäten sprechen

► SB, p. 197

(Lösungsbeispiel)
Great, thank you.
I was at home. / I was in *[dein Urlaubsort]* with my family / my parents / friends / ...
Yes, we were. / No, we weren't. We were on a campsite. / We stayed with friends. / We stayed with my grandparents.

26 Let's talk: Über das Wetter sprechen

► SB, p. 197

1 What was the weather like in Spain? – It was hot and sunny.
2 What's the weather like in Britain in winter? – It's often rainy and cold.

Unit 2: Friends and heroes

1 New words and phrases

► SB, pp. 40–41 | VOCABULARY pp. 208–209

1 straight • **2** braces • **3** glasses • **4** dark • **5** hero • **6** hair • **7** curly • **8** thinks of • **9** heroes

2 New words and phrases

► SB, p. 42 | VOCABULARY p. 209

1 profile • **2** confident • **3** honest • **4** brave • **5** describe; to me

3 New words and phrases

► SB, pp. 43–44 | VOCABULARY p. 209

1 important for/to • **2** agree with • **3** right • **4** on the right; on the left

4 New words and phrases

► SB, p. 46 | VOCABULARY p. 210

1 saved • **2** fall • **3** fell • **4** call • **5** call • **6** (phone) call • **7** hurt

5 New words and phrases

► SB, p. 47 | VOCABULARY p. 210

1 marry • **2** got married • **3** child; children • **4** was born • **5** Leave • **6** left • **7** leave; alone • **8** became

6 New words and phrases

► SB, p. 48 | VOCABULARY pp. 210–211

1 activist • **2** planet • **3** charity

7 New words and phrases

► SB, p. 49 | VOCABULARY p. 211

1 kilometres/km • **2** give • **3** gave • **4** ill • **5** magic

8 Listen carefully!

1 hair • **2** glasses • **3** braces • **4** saving • **5** leave • **6** married • **7** dark • **8** child; children

9 New words and phrases

► SB, p. 50 | VOCABULARY p. 211

1 power • **2** thousand

10 Lost words

1 to • **2** to • **3** for • **4** with • **5** on • **6** into • **7** in • **8** on • **9** of • **10** about • **11** to

11 New words and phrases

► SB, p. 51 | VOCABULARY pp. 211–213

1 any • **2** don't; any • **3** any • **4** boots • **5** silver • **6** helmet • **7** dolphins • **8** man • **9** men • **10** chemicals • **11** swimsuit • **12** earth • **13** strong • **14** nose • **15** trousers • **16** eyes • **17** mask • **18** climb • **19** kill • **20** come with • **21** came • **22** handy • **23** dresses

12 New words and phrases

► SB, p. 52 | VOCABULARY p. 213

1 accident • **2** walls • **3** down • **4** up • **5** landed • **6** dangerous

13 New words and phrases

► SB, p. 53 | VOCABULARY pp. 213–214

1 face • **2** ankle • **3** ambulance • **4** legs • **5** Show • **6** Breathe in • **7** blanket • **8** so (that) • **9** fell asleep • **10** was asleep • **11** jokes

14 New words and phrases

► SB, p. 54 | VOCABULARY p. 214

1 felt • **2** body • **3** fine • **4** broken

15 New words and phrases

► SB, p. 56 | VOCABULARY p. 214

1 work out • **2** languages • **3** false friend

16 New words and phrases

► SB, p. 57 | VOCABULARY pp. 214–215

1 famous for • **2** died • **3** won • **4** discovered • **5** mother; father • **6** fight for • **7** fought • **8** against

17 The fourth word

1 night • **2** feet • **3** children • **4** left

18 Listen carefully!

1 accident • **2** ambulance • **3** swimsuit • **4** chemicals • **5** dangerous • **6** eyes • **7** blanket • **8** languages

19 What's the word?

1 called • **2** dress • **3** landed • **4** plans • **5** surprised • **6** climbed • **7** shows • **8** fight • **9** worry / are worried • **10** tried • **11** laugh

20 Different sounds

1 <u>her</u> • **2** <u>hard</u> • **3** <u>dark</u> • **4** <u>learn</u> • **5** <u>kill</u> • **6** <u>land</u>

21 What did they do?

1 gave • **2** became • **3** left • **4** felt • **5** fought; won • **6** came

22 Let's talk: Sich und andere beschreiben

► SB, p. 195

(Lösungsbeispiel) The person on the left is a girl with curly black hair. She looks quite tall. I think that she's good with computers. The message on her phone tells me that she is a helpful person.
On the right I can see a boy with straight blond hair. He looks quite short. I think that he is good at drawing. I think that he is a very kind boy.

Unit 3: Activities and games

1 New words and phrases
▶ SB, pp. 70–71 | VOCABULARY p. 216

1 theatre • **2** full of • **3** delicious • **4** creative • **5** Insects • **6** actor • **7** acting • **8** 's on • **9** course

2 New words and phrases
▶ SB, p. 72 | VOCABULARY pp. 216–217

1 role-play • **2** practise • **3** practice • **4** real • **5** goat • **6** 're going to; are; going to do • **7** knit • **8** photography • **9** skills • **10** prepare for

3 New words and phrases
▶ SB, p. 73 | VOCABULARY p. 217

1 choose • **2** chose • **3** camera

4 New words and phrases
▶ SB, p. 74 | VOCABULARY p. 217

1 quarter to 7 • **2** quarter past 7 • **3** half past 6

5 Telling the time

1 quarter past 6/six • **2** 8/eight o'clock • **3** half past 3/three • **4** quarter to 10/ten • **5** half past 9/nine • **6** quarter to 7/seven • **7** 1/one o'clock • **8** quarter past 2/two • **9** quarter to 11/eleven

6 New words and phrases
▶ SB, p. 76 | VOCABULARY p. 217

1 classical • **2** acoustic • **3** popular with • **4** than

7 Listen carefully!

1 prepare • **2** photography • **3** camera • **4** actor • **5** theatre • **6** delicious • **7** choose • **8** chose

8 Lost words

1 in • **2** on; at • **3** with • **4** for; on • **5** at; past • **6** to • **7** of • **8** to • **9** to • **10** to

9 New words and phrases
▶ SB, p. 77 | VOCABULARY pp. 217–218

1 as good as • **2** worse • **3** better • **4** like better • **5** relaxing • **6** energetic; energy

10 New words and phrases
▶ SB, pp. 78–79 | VOCABULARY p. 218

1 worst • **2** best • **3** doctor; doctor • **4** at the doctor's • **5** Agent • **6** space • **7** character • **8** take place • **9** took place

11 What's the word?

1 full of • **2** creates • **3** prepare • **4** choose • **5** creative • **6** preparation • **7** chose • **8** goats

12 New words and phrases
▶ SB, p. 80 | VOCABULARY pp. 218–219

1 adventure • **2** bridge • **3** forest • **4** mountain • **5** stairs • **6** key • **7** through • **8** Turn right; turn left • **9** straight on • **10** past the • **11** across

13 New words and phrases
▶ SB, p. 81 | VOCABULARY p. 219

1 trophies • **2** above • **3** above • **4** between • **5** round • **6** the last one • **7** big one; small one • **8** score • **9** bottom • **10** level

14 What's the word: *one* or *ones*?

1 one; one; one; one • **2** ones; ones; ones • **3** ones

15 New words and phrases
▶ SB, p. 82 | VOCABULARY pp. 219–220

1 spends; money on • **2** spent; time with • **3** usually • **4** about • **5** cough • **6** has a headache • **7** go out • **8** click on • **9** screen • **10** rules • **11** an hour a day • **12** until/till • **13** can't/cannot; until/till

16 Plurals

1 children • **2** feet • **3** trophies • **4** pence • **5** noses • **6** men • **7** women • **8** heroes • **9** dresses • **10** keys

17 New words and phrases
▶ SB, pp. 83–84 | VOCABULARY p. 220

1 smiled at • **2** calendar • **3** study • **4** knows • **5** knew • **6** don't use; any more • **7** tips

18 Different sounds

1 fine • **2** learn • **3** than • **4** through • **5** round • **6** wear • **7** cough • **8** go • **9** smile • **10** died

19 Listen carefully!

1 through • **2** left; straight • **3** across; right • **4** bottom • **5** headache • **6** cough • **7** calendar • **8** mountains

20 What's the word?

1 usually • **2** trophies • **3** spends • **4** cough • **5** click

21 Scrambled sentences

1 We often go to the theatre with all the family. • **2** What's on at the cinema at the moment? • **3** I like this song better than the last one. • **4** The dancing competition takes place every summer.

22 New words and phrases
▶ SB, p. 86 | VOCABULARY pp. 220–221

1 opinion • **2** In my opinion • **3** in the world • **4** true • **5** can't; at all • **6** stand • **7** stood

23 Opposites

1 bottom • **2** false • **3** worst • **4** better • **5** (to) be off • **6** out of the house

24 A picture crossword

1 forest • **2** theatre • **3** trophy • **4** mountain • **5** stairs • **6** camera • **7** bridge • **8** calendar • **9** key •**10** goat

25 Let's talk: Sich verabreden: Vorschläge machen und darauf reagieren

▸ p. 196

(Lösungsbeispiel)

Partner A: Can we meet today?
Partner B: Sorry, I can't. I'm really busy today.
Partner A: Are you doing anything special today?
Partner B: I'm helping my parents with the shopping.
Partner A: What are you doing this weekend?
Partner B: I'm not doing anything this weekend.
Partner A: Do you want to come round and have dinner with us this weekend?
Partner B: Oh yes, thank you for the invitation.
Partner A: Would Friday, Saturday or Sunday be best?
Partner B: Saturday would be best.

26 Let's talk: Seine Meinung äußern und diskutieren

▸ p. 198

1 (I'm sorry,) I don't agree.
2 What do you think?
3 That looks really interesting.
4 That's not a good idea.

Unit 4: Celebrate!

1 New words and phrases

▸ SB, pp. 98–99 | VOCABULARY pp. 221–222

1 celebrates • **2** celebration • **3** fireworks • **4** throw • **5** threw • **6** throw away • **7** carnival • **8** breaking; fast • **9** broke • **10** Easter • **11** Christmas • **12** biscuit • **13** candles

2 New words and phrases

▸ SB, pp. 100–101 | VOCABULARY p. 222

1 during • **2** pray • **3** Thank • **4** god • **5** mosque • **6** hope

3 New words and phrases

▸ SB, pp. 102–103 | VOCABULARY p. 222

1 sell; buy • **2** sold; bought • **3** a little • **4** a few • **5** almost • **6** Yoghurt • **7** lamb • **8** May I • **9** onion • **10** dictionary

4 New words and phrases

▸ SB, pp. 104–105 | VOCABULARY p. 223

1 wedding • **2** nervous • **3** have practised • **4** haven't practised • **5** have; done • **6** not; yet • **7** yet • **8** finishes • **9** ever • **10** the best teacher ever • **11** Have; been to • **12** have; eaten • **13** Have; seen • **14** have met • **15** have given • **16** Have; swum • **17** haven't won; yet

5 New words and phrases

▸ SB, p. 106 | VOCABULARY pp. 223–224

1 just • **2** I've come / I have come • **3** hasn't come • **4** chores • **5** soon • **6** mustn't • **7** vacuum • **8** vacuum cleaner • **9** takes out • **10** set • **11** set the table • **12** set the table

6 What are the words: *must – mustn't – don't have to*?

1 don't have to • **2** must • **3** mustn't • **4** don't have to • **5** mustn't • **6** must

7 New words and phrases

▸ SB, p. 107 | VOCABULARY p. 224

1 lonely • **2** At least • **3** stepson; stepdaughter

8 What have they already done? What haven't they done?

1 done; yet • **2** finished; started; yet • **3** already eaten • **4** met: yet • **5** found; yet • **6** already bought

9 Listen carefully!

1 celebrated • **2** celebration • **3** fireworks • **4** biscuits • **5** lamb • **6** yoghurt • **7** finished • **8** ever

10 New words and phrases

▸ SB, pp. 108–109 | VOCABULARY pp. 224–225

1 member • **2** rhymes • **3** tradition • **4** traditional • **5** poems • **6** onto the table • **7** knock at • **8** knocked over • **9** sang • **10** sounds

11 Lost words

1 to • **2** during • **3** at • **4** of • **5** in • **6** out • **7** at • **8** to • **9** onto; over

12 What's the word?

1 rhymes • **2** score • **3** sound • **4** finished • **5** hope • **6** smile

13 New words and phrases

▸ SB, p. 110 | VOCABULARY p. 225

1 on time • **2** excited • **3** Put; on • **4** took off • **5** beautiful • **6** wear • **7** wore • **8** has; worn • **9** suits

14 Different sounds

1 card; day • **2** done; dog • **3** tall; castle • **4** soon; round

15 New words and phrases

▸ SB, p. 111 | VOCABULARY pp. 225–226

1 Have; taken • **2** Just then • **3** just there • **4** slippers • **5** as/when • **6** terrible • **7** still • **8** could; could

16 New words and phrases

▸ SB, p. 112 | VOCABULARY p. 226

1 jacket • **2** multicultural • **3** scarf • **4** scarves • **5** shirt

17 New words and phrases

▸ SB, p. 114 | VOCABULARY p. 226

1 along the river • **2** church • **3** All over the world • **4** mirror

18 Listen carefully!

1 wedding • **2** multicultural • **3** mosque • **4** beautiful • **5** suit • **6** excited • **7** stepdaughter • **8** traditional

19 A picture crossword

1 biscuit • **2** mirror • **3** church • **4** jacket • **5** mosque • **6** yoghurt • **7** onion • **8** candle • **9** suit • **10** slippers

20 Let's talk: Beim Essen und bei Tisch

▸ SB, pp. 196–197

(Lösungsbeispiel)

1 Can I have some orange juice, please?
2 Can I have some salad, please?
3 Would you like some potatoes?
4 Yes, please.
5 Enjoy your meal!

21 Let's talk: Feedback geben

▸ SB, p. 199

(Lösungsbeispiel)

1 Great job!
2 I understood most of what you said.
3 You looked at the class.
4 Try to speak loudly and clearly.
5 You smiled.
6 Your pictures were too small.

Unit 5: Getting ready for the future

1 New words and phrases

▸ SB, pp. 128–129 | VOCABULARY p. 227

1 future • **2** future • **3** fix • **4** sick • **5** sickness • **6** artist • **7** firefighter • **8** hairdresser • **9** at the hairdresser's • **10** mechanic • **11** nurse • **12** plumber • **13** programmer; programs • **14** program • **15** anybody/anyone • **16** don't know anybody / don't know anyone • **17** as a teacher

2 New words and phrases

▸ SB, pp. 130–131 | VOCABULARY p. 228

1 mind • **2** can't make up my mind • **3** I want to be a firefighter. • **4** especially • **5** Perhaps • **6** business • **7** business owner • **8** have started a business • **9** own • **10** architect • **11** teaches • **13** taught

3 Word partners

1 sickness – illness • **2** anybody – anyone • **3** perhaps – maybe • **4** a little – a bit • **5** (to) finish – (to) end • **6** terrible – horrible

4 New words and phrases

▸ SB, pp. 132–133 | VOCABULARY pp. 228–229

1 I'll be / I will be • **2** won't / will not • **3** anything • **4** can't see anything • **5** respect for • **6** Do; believe in • **7** predictions • **8** earns • **9** hard-working • **10** rich • **11** successful

5 What are their jobs?

1 plumber • **2** nurse • **3** artist/painter • **4** car mechanic • **5** hairdresser • **6** programmer • **7** architect • **8** firefighter

6 New words and phrases

▸ SB, pp. 134–135 | VOCABULARY p. 229

1 noticed • **2** does the washing • **3** Fold • **4** look after • **5** Look at • **6** Look for • **7** Look; up • **8** babysit • **9** babysat • **10** babysitting • **11** empty; dishwasher • **12** hate • **13** least • **14** at least

7 Listen carefully!

1 future • **2** predictions • **3** nurse • **4** earn • **5** successful • **6** business • **7** chores • **8** dishwasher

8 New words and phrases

► SB, p. 136 | VOCABULARY pp. 229–230

1 treat • **2** pocket money • **3** magazines • **4** shop • **5** stuff • **6** (in) cash • **7** by card • **8** cash machine • **9** gift • **10** gift shop • **11** savings account • **12** bank • **13** coins • **14** piggy bank

9 New words and phrases

► SB, p. 137 | VOCABULARY pp. 230–231

1 bakery • **2** Bakers • **3** bake • **4** electronics • **5** newsagent • **6** newsagent's

10 New words and phrases

► SB, p. 138 | VOCABULARY p. 231

1 size • **2** large • **3** price • **4** prize • **5** How much is • **6** How much are • **7** change • **8** those • **9** try on

11 New words and phrases

► SB, p. 139 | VOCABULARY p. 232

1 shop assistant • **2** each • **3** customer • **4** Would you like anything else?

12 Lost words

1 at • **2** on • **3** about • **4** in • **5** at • **6** after • **7** in; by • **8** for • **9** for • **10** for; of

13 New words and phrases

► SB, pp. 140 141 | VOCABULARY p. 232

1 sell; buy • **2** have sold • **3** move to • **4** miss • **5** hug • **6** Do; hug • **7** each other • **8** work experience

14 New words and phrases

► SB, p. 142 | VOCABULARY pp. 232–233

1 repeat • **2** contact • **3** strength • **4** strong • **5** solve

15 Listen carefully!

1 sold • **2** price • **3** savings account • **4** bakery • **5** cash machine • **6** repeat • **7** strengths • **8** work experience

16 New words and phrases

► SB, p. 144 | VOCABULARY p. 233

1 Dear • **2** How are you? • **3** looks forward to • **4** look forward to hearing • **5** Take care. • **6** understands • **7** understood

17 New words and phrases

► SB, p. 145 | VOCABULARY p. 233

1 horoscopes • **2** star sign • **3** useful • **4** realistic

18 Picture crossword

1 trousers • **2** braces • **3** stairs • **4** clothes • **5** glasses • **6** magazine • **7** coin • **8** newsagent's • **9** cash machine • **10** bakery • **11** piggy bank • **12** nurse • **13** dishwasher

19 Let's talk: Über Berufe und die Zukunft sprechen

▸ SB, p. 198

(Lösungsbeispiel)

When I was little, I wanted to be a teacher / a firefighter / a ... Now I want to be a computer programmer / a nurse / a ... My mum is a shop assistant / a designer / a singer / a ... My dad is a builder / a driver / a dancer / a ... In the future I'll have a wife/husband and two children. Perhaps I'll have a house in the country.

20 Let's talk: Einkaufen und über Preise sprechen

▸ SB, p. 199

(Lösungsbeispiel)

Bild 1:

A: Can **I help you**?
B: Yes, please. Do you **have these trousers in size M**?
A: I'll go and see if we have them in size M. What about the dress?
B: Do you have **it in blue**?
A: Here you are.
B: Thank you. Can I **try them on**?
A: Yes, of course, the changing rooms are over there.

Bild 2:

C: How would you like to pay?
B: I'd like **to pay (in) cash**.
C: OK. That's £ 125.98.
B: I'd **like a bag**, please.
C: No problem, and here's your **change**.
B: **Thank you. Goodbye.**
C: Bye.

15 New words and phrases

▸ SB, p. 82 | VOCABULARY pp. 219–220

1	Sam ____________ a lot of ____________ computer games.	Sam **gibt** viel **Geld für** Computerspiele **aus.**
2	When she was little, Dilek ____________ a lot of ________ ________ her cousins.	Als sie klein war, **verbrachte** Dilek viel **Zeit mit** ihren Kusinen.
3	Tom is ____________ at home in the evening.	Tom ist abends **meistens** zu Hause.
4	He goes to bed at ____________ ten o'clock.	Er geht **ungefähr** um zehn Uhr ins Bett.
5	The baby has a bad ____________.	Das Baby hat einen schlimmen **Husten.**
6	Tom can't do sport today because he ________ ____________.	Tom kann heute keinen Sport machen, da er **Kopfschmerzen hat.**
7	Tom is unhappy because he can't ________ ____________ with his friends.	Tom ist unglücklich, weil er nicht mit seinen Freunden **rausgehen** kann.
8	If you need more information, ________ ____________ the link.	Wenn Sie weitere Informationen benötigen, **klicken** Sie **auf** den Link.
9	I don't watch films on my phone because the ____________ is too small.	Ich schaue keine Filme auf meinem Handy, weil der **Bildschirm** zu klein ist.
10	I don't know the ____________ of rugby.	Ich kenne die Rugby-**Regeln** nicht.
11	Molly only watches TV ____________ ____________.	Molly sieht nur **eine Stunde pro Tag** fern.
12	She can watch TV ____________ her mother comes home.	Sie kann fernsehen, **bis** ihre Mutter nach Hause kommt.
13	We ____________ play outside ____________ the rain stops.	Wir **können erst** draußen spielen, **wenn** der Regen aufhört.

16 Plurals

Sieh dir die Wörter an und schreibe die Mehrzahl auf.

1 child – ____________

2 foot – ____________

3 trophy – ____________

4 penny – ____________

5 nose – ____________

6 man – ____________

7 woman – ____________

8 hero – ____________

9 dress – ____________

10 key – ____________

▸ Check

17 New words and phrases

▸ SB, pp. 83–84 | VOCABULARY p. 220

	English	Deutsch
1	The baby __________ his father.	Das Baby **lächelte** seinen Vater **an**.
2	"Are you free on Tuesday?" – "Let me check my __________."	„Hast du am Dienstag Zeit?" – „Lass mich meinen **Kalender** checken."
3	Tom wants to __________ art.	Tom möchte Kunst **studieren**.
4	Tom __________ a lot about art.	Tom **weiß** viel über Kunst.
5	"John was late again." – "I __________ it!"	„John kam wieder zu spät." – „Ich **wusste** es!"
6	This phone is very old. I __________ it __________.	Das Handy ist sehr alt. Ich **benutze** es **nicht mehr**.
7	Can you give me some __________ for buying a mobile phone?	Kannst du mir ein paar **Tipps** für den Kauf eines Handys geben?

18 Different sounds

Welcher Vokallaut klingt anders als die anderen in der Reihe? Unterstreiche das Wort.

1 knit – skill – fine – tip
2 real – meal – hear – learn
3 half – than – past – fast
4 cough – wash – through – dog
5 rule – true – through – round
6 worse – were – learn – wear
7 round – now – cough – house
8 cough – on – wrong – go
9 trip – smile – bridge – till
10 screen – treat – key – died

19 Listen carefully!

07

Höre dir die Sätze aufmerksam an und schreibe das fehlende Wort in die Lücke.

1 Let's walk __________ the park.
2 Turn __________ at the cinema and then go __________ on.
3 Walk __________ Station Road and turn __________ into Theatre Street.
4 Our house is at the __________ of the street.
5 Sally can't go to school today because she has a __________.
6 Sally's brother has a bad __________.
7 Please check your __________ to see if you're free on Tuesday.
8 We were on a nice campsite in the __________.

▸ Check

20 What's the word?

Vervollständige die Sätze mit den Wörtern aus dem Kasten. Achte auf die Form.

click • cough • spend • trophy • usually

1 Peter ____________ cycles to work, but when it rains, he takes the bus.

2 Sarah's football team won two ____________ last year.

3 Tim ____________ a lot of money on books.

4 Rula has a ____________ and a headache and can't go to school today.

5 Think hard before you ____________ on a link!

21 Scrambled sentences

Hier sind die Wörter in den Sätzen durcheinandergeraten. Bringe sie in die richtige Reihenfolge.

often · to · theatre · go · with · the · the · We · family · all

1 ____________

cinema · at · the · What's · on · at the moment?

2 ____________

this · last · song · better · than · I · the · one · like

3 ____________

competition · summer · takes · place · The · every · dancing

4 ____________

22 New words and phrases

► SB, p. 86 | VOCABULARY pp. 220–221

1	What's your ____________ on homework?	Was ist deine **Meinung** zu Hausaufgaben?
2	____________ they're helpful.	**Meiner Meinung nach** sind sie hilfreich.
3	What's the best place ____________ for you?	Was ist der beste Platz **auf der Welt** für dich?
4	Is it ____________ that you bought a house?	Ist es **wahr**, dass du ein Haus gekauft hast?
5	Where are you? I ____________ see you ____________.	Wo bist du? Ich **kann** dich **gar nicht** sehen.
6	I feel too ill to ____________ here.	Ich fühle mich zu krank, um hier zu **stehen**.
7	Tom ____________ next to Molly.	Tom **stand** neben Molly.

23 Opposites

Finde die Gegenteile.

1 top ◄► ______________________
2 true ◄► ______________________
3 best ◄► ______________________
4 worse ◄► ______________________
5 (to) be on ◄► ______________________
6 into the house ◄► ______________________

24 A picture crossword

Sieh dir die Bilder an und trage die richtigen Wörter in das Gitter ein.

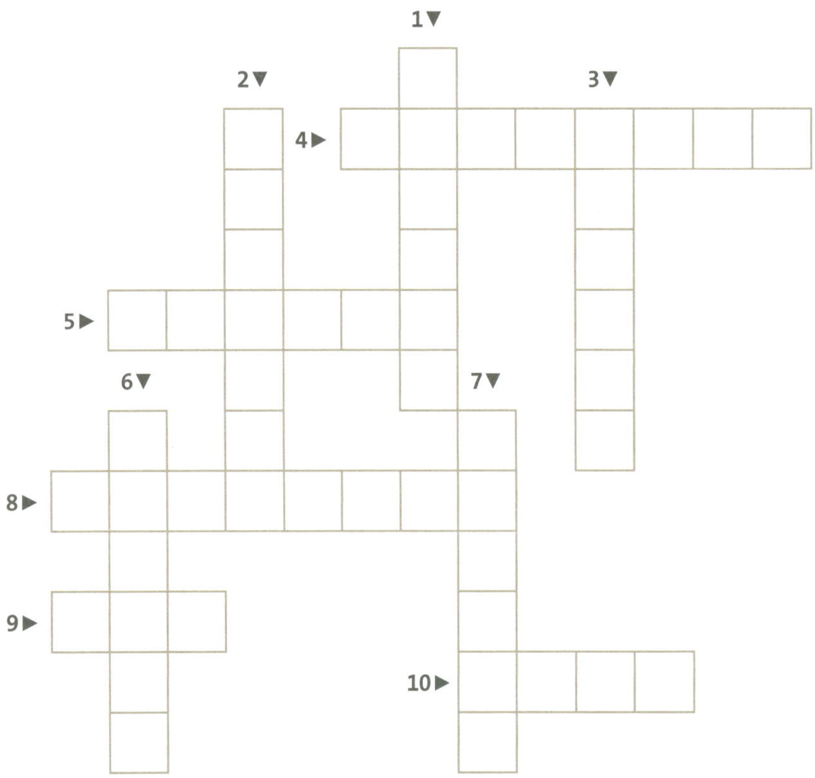

1 

2 

3 

4 

5 

6 

7 

8 

9 

10 

► Check

25 Let's talk: Sich verabreden: Vorschläge machen und darauf reagieren

▸ SB, p. 196

Partner A möchte sich mit Partner B verabreden. Schreibe ihren Dialog mit den Sätzen aus dem Kasten in dein Heft. Du kannst deinen Dialog auch aufnehmen und jemanden bitten, ihn sich anzuhören und dir Feedback zu geben.

I'm helping my parents with the shopping. • Saturday would be best. • Oh yes, thanks for the invitation. • Do you want to come round and have dinner with us this weekend? • I'm not doing anything this weekend. • Sorry, I can't. • Would Friday, Saturday or Sunday be best? • Are you doing anything special today? • ~~Can we meet today?~~ • I'm really busy today. • What are you doing this weekend?

26 Let's talk: Seine Meinung äußern und diskutieren

▸ SB, p. 198

Sieh dir die Fragen unten an und beantworte sie. Du kannst deine Antworten auch aufnehmen und jemanden bitten, sie sich anzuhören und dir Feedback zu geben.

Was sagst du auf Englisch, wenn ...

1 ... du sagen möchtest, dass du anderer Meinung bist?

____

2 ... du fragen möchtest, was dein/e Gesprächspartner/in über eine Sache denkt?

____

3 ... du sagen möchtest, dass etwas sehr interessant aussieht?

____

4 ... du sagen möchtest, dass etwas keine gute Idee ist?

____

Unit 4
Celebrate!

1 New words and phrases

▸ SB, pp. 98–99 | VOCABULARY pp. 221–222

1	Tom ____________ his birthday every year.	Tom **feiert** jedes Jahr seinen Geburtstag.
2	Tom spends a lot of time preparing his ____________.	Tom verbringt viel Zeit damit, seine **Feier** vorzubereiten.
3	There is a ____________ competition in our town every summer.	In unserer Stadt gibt es jeden Sommer einen **Feuerwerks**wettbewerb.
4	Why do you ____________ your clothes on the floor? Put them in your wardrobe.	Warum **wirfst** du deine Klamotten auf den Fußboden? Leg sie in deinen Schrank.
5	Tom ____________ the ball over the wall.	Tom **warf** den Ball über die Mauer.
6	Can I ____________ these boxes or do you still need them?	Kann ich diese Kisten **wegwerfen**, oder brauchst du sie noch?
7	Zola makes her own ____________ costumes.	Zola macht ihre **Karnevals**kostüme selbst.
8	We enjoy ____________ the ____________ with all the family.	Wir genießen das **Fastenbrechen** mit der ganzen Familie.
9	The wind was so strong last night that my bedroom window ____________.	Der Wind war so stark letzte Nacht, dass mein Schlafzimmerfenster **zerbrochen ist**.
10	John visits his grandparents at ____________.	John besucht seine Großeltern zu **Ostern**.
11	How do you celebrate ____________?	Wie feiert ihr **Weihnachten**?
12	Would you like a ____________?	Möchtest du einen **Keks**?
13	We put real ____________ on our Christmas tree.	Wir stecken echte **Kerzen** an unseren Weihnachtsbaum.

▸ Check

2 New words and phrases

▸ SB, pp. 100–101 | VOCABULARY p. 222

1	Don't talk ________________ a concert.	Sprich nicht **während** eines Konzerts.
2	Let's ________________ for this war to stop.	Lasst uns dafür **beten**, dass dieser Krieg endet.
3	________________ Grandma for the present.	**Bedanke** dich bei Oma für das Geschenk.
4	Neptun is the ________________ of the sea.	Neptun ist der **Gott** des Meeres.
5	Farid and his father pray at the ________________ on Fridays.	Farid und sein Vater beten freitags in der **Moschee**.
6	I ________________ you get well soon.	Ich **hoffe**, dass du bald wieder gesund bist.

3 New words and phrases

▸ SB, pp. 102–103 | VOCABULARY p. 222

1	I want to ________________ my old bike and ________________ a better one.	Ich möchte mein altes Fahrrad **verkaufen** und mir ein besseres **kaufen**.
2	We ________________ our small house last year and ________________ a bigger one.	Wir **haben** unser kleines Haus letztes Jahr **verkauft** und ein größeres **gekauft**.
3	I only take ________________ sugar in my coffee.	Ich nehme nur **ein bisschen** Zucker in meinen Kaffee.
4	I need ________________ things from the supermarket.	Ich brauche **ein paar** Sachen aus dem Supermarkt.
5	I have to go home now. It's ________________ dark.	Ich muss jetzt nach Hause gehen. Es ist schon **fast** dunkel.
6	"What's for dessert?" – "________________ fruit."	„Was gibt es zum Nachtisch?" – „**Joghurt** und Obst."
7	Our main course today is ________________ or chicken.	Unser Hauptgericht heute ist **Lammfleisch** oder Hühnchen.
8	________________ watch TV this evening?	**Darf ich** heute Abend fernsehen?
9	Do you like French ________________ soup?	Magst du französische **Zwiebel**suppe?
10	If you don't know a word in another language, you can look it up in a ________________.	Wenn du ein Wort einer anderen Sprache nicht kennst, kannst du es in einem **Wörterbuch** nachschlagen.

▸ Check

4 New words and phrases

▸ SB, pp. 104–105 | VOCABULARY p. 223

	English	Deutsch
1	Yara and Joe's ____________ was wonderful.	Yara und Joes **Hochzeit** war wunderbar.
2	Joe was very ____________.	Joe war sehr **nervös**.
3	I ____________ the guitar for two hours.	Ich **habe** zwei Stunden Gitarre **geübt**.
4	I'm worried because I ____________ ____________ my presentation.	Ich mache mir Sorgen, weil ich meine Präsentation **nicht geübt habe**.
5	John, you look unhappy. What ____________ you ____________?	John, du siehst traurig aus. Was **hast** du **getan**?
6	The lesson has ____________ started ____________.	Die Unterrichtsstunde hat **noch nicht** begonnen.
7	Have you done your homework ____________?	Hast du **schon** deine Hausaufgaben gemacht?
8	The school concert ____________ at 9 o'clock.	Das Schulkonzert **endet** um 21 Uhr.
9	Have you ____________ played tennis?	Hast du **schon einmal** Tennis gespielt?
10	All the students say that Ms Black is ____________ ____________.	Alle Schüler/innen finden, dass Frau Black **die beste Lehrerin ist, die man sich wünschen kann**.
11	____________ you ever ____________ ____________ Brighton?	**Bist** du schon einmal **in** Brighton **gewesen**?
12	I ____________ never ____________ lamb.	Ich **habe** noch nie Lammfleisch **gegessen.**
13	____________ you ____________ my dog?	**Hast** du meinen Hund **gesehen**?
14	I ____________ our new neighbours. They're very nice.	Ich **habe** unsere neuen Nachbarn **getroffen**. Sie sind sehr nett.
15	I ____________ them my phone number.	Ich **habe** ihnen meine Telefonnummer **gegeben.**
16	____________ you ever ____________ in a river?	**Bist** du jemals in einem Fluss **geschwommen**?
17	I ____________ a prize ____________.	Ich **habe noch keinen** Preis **gewonnen**.

▸ Check

5 New words and phrases

▶ SB, p. 106 | VOCABULARY pp. 223–224

	English	Deutsch
1	I've ____________ seen the best film ever.	Ich habe **gerade** den besten Film aller Zeiten gesehen.
2	Hi Tarek, ____________ to help you.	Hi Tarek, **ich bin gekommen**, um dir zu helfen.
3	Tom is worried about Molly because she ____________ home yet.	Tom macht sich Sorgen um Molly, weil sie noch **nicht** nach Hause **gekommen ist.**
4	What ____________ do you do at home?	Welche **Pflichten** erledigst du zu Hause?
5	We're going to move ____________.	Wir ziehen **bald** um.
6	You ____________ hit other children.	Du **darfst** andere Kinder **nicht** schlagen.
7	Can you ____________ the living room, please?	Kannst du bitte im Wohnzimmer **Staub saugen**?
8	We need a new ____________.	Wir brauchen einen neuen **Staubsauger**.
9	Tom ____________ the rubbish every morning.	Tom **bringt** jeden Morgen den Müll **raus**.
10	My dog eats everything that I ____________ in front of him.	Mein Hund frisst alles, was ich vor ihn **stelle**.
11	Please ____________.	Bitte **deck den Tisch**.
12	My grandpa never ____________. Grandma always did it.	Mein Großvater **hat** nie **den Tisch gedeckt**. Das hat immer Großmutter gemacht.

6 What are the words: *must – mustn't – don't have to?*

Setze die richtigen Wörter in die Sätze ein.

1 You ____________ walk the dog. I've already been in the park with him.

2 You ____________ buy a ticket before you get on the bus.

3 You ____________ eat sweets after you have brushed your teeth.

4 You ____________ be successful as long as you're happy.

5 You ____________ leave the door open when you leave the house.

6 You ____________ finish your homework before you can watch TV.

7 New words and phrases

► SB, p. 107 | VOCABULARY p. 224

1 Tarek has no brothers or sisters. Sometimes he feels ____________.	Tarek hat keine Geschwister. Manchmal fühlt er sich **einsam**.
2 ____________ he has lots of friends.	**Wenigstens** hat er viele Freunde.
3 Sally has a ____________ and a ____________.	Sally hat einen **Stiefsohn** und eine **Stieftochter**.

8 What have they already done? What haven't they done yet?

► SB, p. 271 (irregular verbs)

Vervollständige die Aussagesätze und Fragen mit dem *past participle* des Verbs in Klammern und *already* oder *yet*.

1 Have you ____________ (do) your homework ____________?

2 I've ____________ (finish) maths, but I haven't ____________ (start) my art presentation ____________.

3 I'm not hungry. I've ____________ (eat).

4 I haven't ____________ (meet) my new neighbours ____________.

5 Have you ____________ (find) your phone ____________?

6 It's Lisa's birthday next week. I've ____________ (buy) a nice present for her.

9 Listen carefully!

08

Höre dir die Sätze aufmerksam an und schreibe das fehlende Wort in die Lücke.

1 Grandpa ____________ his 80th birthday last Saturday.

2 It was a very special ____________.

3 We even had ____________ in the evening.

4 In the afternoon we had ____________ and chocolates.

5 In the evening we ate beef and ____________ with potatoes and vegetables.

6 There was also ____________ with fruit.

7 The party ____________ at 11 o'clock.

8 It was the best party ____________!

► Check

10 New words and phrases

▶ SB, pp. 108–109 | VOCABULARY pp. 224–225

1	Lara is a ________________ of a tennis club.	Lara ist **Mitglied** in einem Tennisverein.
2	*'True'* ________________ with *'new'*.	‚*True*' **reimt sich** auf ‚*new*'.
3	Eating chocolate eggs at Easter is a ________________ in Britain and Germany.	Ostern Schokoladeneier zu essen ist eine **Tradition** in Großbritannien und Deutschland.
4	Our band plays ________________ Irish music.	Unsere Band spielt **traditionelle** irische Musik.
5	Sina sometimes writes ________________.	Sina schreibt manchmal **Gedichte**.
6	Don't let the cat jump ________________ ________________.	Lass die Katze nicht **auf den Tisch** springen.
7	Please ________________ my door before you come into my room.	Bitte **klopf an**, bevor du in mein Zimmer kommst.
8	The little boy ________________ the jar.	Der kleine Junge **stieß** das Glas **um**.
9	The singer ________________ all my favourite songs.	Die Band **hat** alle meine Lieblingslieder **gesungen**.
10	A picnic with all the family ________________ nice.	Ein Picknick mit der ganzen Familie **klingt** gut.

11 Lost words

Vervollständige die Sätze mit den Wörtern aus den Luftballons.

1 Moira has invited me *to* her birthday party.

2 Don't look at your phone __________ the concert.

3 The concert finishes __________ 9 o'clock.

4 The band played lots __________ traditional songs.

5 A lot of people have been ill __________ the last few weeks.

6 Can you take __________ the rubbish, please?

7 Please knock __________ my door before you come in.

8 Have you ever been __________ London?

9 A big cat jumped __________ the table and knocked __________ a glass of water.

12 What's the word?

**Vervollständige die Sätze mit den Wörtern aus dem Kasten.
Achte dabei auf die Wortart und die richtige Form des Wortes.**

finish • hope • rhyme • score • smile • sound

1 *'Pound'* ________________ with *'sound'*.

2 How many points did you ________________?

3 There was a strange ________________ in the garden.

4 Tim ________________ school last year.

5 Sarah hasn't found a job yet, but she hasn't given up ________________ to find one.

6 Ms Berry always has a ________________ on her face.

13 New words and phrases

▸ SB, p. 110 | VOCABULARY p. 225

1 The concert started ________________.	Das Konzert begann **pünktlich**.
2 It was Molly's first concert. She was very ________________.	Es war Mollys erstes Konzert. Sie war sehr **aufgeregt**.
3 ________ your shoes ________. We're leaving.	**Zieh** deine Schuhe **an**. Wir gehen.
4 Sam ________________ his hat.	Sam **legte** den Hut **ab**.
5 Paul has a ________________ garden.	Paul hat einen **wunderschönen** Garten.
6 British students usually ________________ school uniforms.	Britische Schüler/innen **tragen** normalerweise Schuluniformen.
7 Mary only ________________ dresses when she was little.	Mary **trug** nur Kleider, als sie klein war.
8 Tarek ________ never ________ a hat.	Tarek **hat** nie einen Hut **getragen**.
9 Jake likes wearing blue ________________.	Jake trägt gern blaue **Anzüge**.

14 Different sounds

**Welcher Vokallaut klingt anders als die anderen in der Reihe?
Unterstreiche das Wort.
Suche dann zu jeder Reihe ein passendes Wort im Kasten.**

castle • day • dog • round

1 pray – place – card – cape ________________

2 god – knock – shop – done ________________

3 ask – arm – tall – calm ________________

4 sound – down – proud – soon ________________

▸ Check

15 New words and phrases

► SB, p. 111 | VOCABULARY pp. 225–226

1 ________ you ________ your swimsuit?	**Hast** du deinen Badeanzug **mitgenommen**?
2 We arrived in the park. ________________ it started to rain.	Wir kamen im Park an. **Genau dann** fing es zu regnen an.
3 Our old house was ________________, next to the supermarket.	Unser altes Haus war **genau dort**, neben dem Supermarkt.
4 Put your ________________ on, please.	Zieh bitte deine **Hausschuhe** an.
5 The girls laughed ________ they danced.	Die Mädchen lachten, **während** sie tanzten.
6 Joe had a ________________ dream.	Joe hatte einen **schrecklichen** Traum.
7 The house is expensive, but we ________________ want to buy it.	Das Haus ist teuer, aber wir wollen es **trotzdem** kaufen.
8 We ________________ ask our parents. Maybe they ________________ help us.	Wir **könnten** unsere Eltern fragen. Vielleicht **könnten** sie uns helfen.

16 New words and phrases

► SB, p. 112 | VOCABULARY p. 226

1 It's cold outside. You need a ________________.	Es ist kalt draußen. Du brauchst eine **Jacke**.
2 Joe lives in a ________________ neighbourhood.	Joe wohnt in einem **multikulturellen** Stadtteil.
3 I always wear a ________________ in winter.	Im Winter trage ich immer einen **Schal**.
4 I have lots of different ________________.	Ich habe viele verschiedene **Schals**.
5 Please put on a clean ________________.	Bitte zieh ein sauberes **Hemd** an.

17 New words and phrases

► SB, p. 114 | VOCABULARY p. 226

1 I often cycle ________________________.	Ich radle oft **den Fluss entlang**.
2 The Millers go to ________________ on Sundays.	Die Millers gehen sonntags in die **Kirche**.
3 ________________________, people like music.	**Überall auf der Welt** mögen die Menschen Musik. 
4 We have a big ________________ in our bathroom.	Wir haben einen großen **Spiegel** im Badezimmer.

18 Listen carefully!

09

Höre dir die Sätze aufmerksam an und schreibe das fehlende Wort in die Lücke.

1 My friend has invited me to his ____________________.

2 My friend comes from a ____________________ family.

3 I've never been in a ____________________.

4 My friend lives in a ____________________ house.

5 I have to buy a new ____________________.

6 Tom is ____________________ about his school trip.

7 John's ____________________ sings in a band.

8 She likes ____________________ songs.

19 A picture crossword

Sieh dir die Bilder an und trage die richtigen Wörter in das Gitter ein.

1

2

3

4

5

6

7

8

9

10

▸ Check

20 Let's talk: Beim Essen und bei Tisch

▸ SB, pp. 196–197

Sieh dir das Bild an und schreibe passende Fragen und Antworten in die Sprechblasen.

21 Let's talk: Feedback geben

▸ SB, p. 199

Ein/e Klassenkamerad/in hat eine Präsentation auf Englisch gehalten. Welches Feedback kannst du ihm/ihr im Anschluss daran auf Englisch geben? Schreibe es auf die jeweilige Zeile.

1 Sehr gut gemacht: ____________________

2 Ich habe das meiste, was du gesagt hast, verstanden: ____________________

____

3 Du hast die Klasse angesehen: ____________________

4 Versuche, laut und deutlich zu sprechen: ____________________

5 Du hast gelächelt: ____________________

6 Deine Bilder waren zu klein: ____________________

Unit 5
Getting ready for the future

1 New words and phrases

▸ SB, pp. 128–129 | VOCABULARY p. 227

1	Let's work together in the ________________.	Lass uns in **Zukunft** zusammenarbeiten.
2	Joe and his ________________ wife met at school.	Joe und seine **zukünftige** Ehefrau haben sich in der Schule kennengelernt.
3	Dad, can you ________________ my bike, please?	Papa, kannst du bitte mein Fahrrad **reparieren**?
4	A ________________ child can't go to school.	Ein **krankes** Kind kann nicht zur Schule gehen.
5	Travel ________________ is something horrible.	Reise**krankheit** ist etwas Schreckliches.
6	Pete is an ________________. He draws great pictures.	Pete ist **Künstler**. Er zeichnet tolle Bilder.
7	Joe is a ________________.	Joe ist **Feuerwehrmann**.
8	Joe's brother is a ________________.	Joes Bruder ist **Friseur**.
9	Tarek is not at home. He's ________________ ________________.	Tarek ist nicht zu Hause. Er ist **beim Friseur**.
10	Joe's wife is a car ________________.	Joes Ehefrau ist Auto**mechanikerin**.
11	Joe's mother is a ________________.	Joes Mutter ist **Krankenpflegerin**.
12	Joe's father is a ________________.	Joes Vater ist **Sanitärinstallateur**.
13	A ________________ writes computer ________________.	Ein/e **Programmierer/in** schreibt Computer**programme**.
14	Could you ________________ my new mobile phone for me?	Könntest du mein neues Handy für mich **programmieren**?
15	Do you know ________________ who can help me to fix my bike?	Kennst du **irgendjemanden**, der mir helfen kann, mein Fahrrad zu reparieren?
16	No, I ________________________ who could help you.	Nein, ich **kenne niemanden**, der dir helfen könnte.
17	Lynn works ________________ in Berlin.	Lynn arbeitet **als Lehrerin** in Berlin.

▸ Check

2 New words and phrases

► SB, pp. 130–131 | VOCABULARY p. 228

	English	Deutsch
1	He's forty years old but sometimes has the ________________ of a four-year-old.	Er ist vierzig Jahre alt, hat aber manchmal den **Verstand** eines Vierjährigen.
2	"Do you want to join a football club?" – "I ________________________________."	„Möchtest du in eine Fußballmannschaft gehen?" – „Ich **kann mich nicht entscheiden**."
3	________________________________ ________________.	**Ich möchte Feuerwehrmann/Feuerwehrfrau werden.**
4	I love fruit, ________________ strawberries.	Ich liebe Obst, **insbesondere** Erdbeeren.
5	"I can't find my keys." – "________________ you've left them at home."	„Ich kann meine Schlüssel nicht finden." – „**Vielleicht** hast du sie zu Hause gelassen."
6	Rishi's parents have their own ________________.	Rishis Eltern haben ihren eigenen **Betrieb**.
7	One day Rishi wants to be a ________________ ________________ too.	Eines Tages möchte auch Rishi **Geschäftsinhaber** sein.
8	Alfie and Thomas ________________________ ________________________________.	Alfie und Thomas **haben einen Betrieb gegründet**.
9	The Millers ________________ three houses.	Die Millers **besitzen** drei Häuser.
10	As an ________________ you need to be good at maths and drawing.	Als **Architekt/in** musst du gut in Mathematik und Zeichnen sein.
11	Ms Hall ________________ French.	Frau Hall **unterrichtet** Französisch.
12	Tom's father ________________ German.	Toms Vater **unterrichtete** Deutsch.

3 Word partners

Verbinde die Wörter und Ausdrücke, die zusammenpassen.

sickness · anybody · perhaps · a little · (to) finish · terrible

maybe · a bit · (to) end · horrible · illness · anyone

(Example: sickness – illness)

► Check

4 New words and phrases

▸ SB, pp. 132–133 | VOCABULARY pp. 228–229

1	In 2040 ________________ thirty years old.	2040 **werde ich** dreißig Jahre alt **sein**.
2	You ________________ believe me, but I really like going to school.	Du **wirst** mir **nicht** glauben, aber ich gehe wirklich gern zur Schule.
3	Do you want ________________ from the market?	Möchtest du **irgendetwas** vom Markt?
4	It's so dark here. I ______________________ ________________.	Es ist so dunkel hier. Ich **kann nichts sehen**.
5	I have a lot of ________________ nurses.	Ich habe viel **Respekt vor** Krankenpflegern.
6	_______ you ________________ god?	**Glaubst** du **an** Gott?
7	It's difficult to make ________________ about the future of our youth centre.	Es ist schwierig, **Vorhersagen** über die Zukunft unseres Jugendzentrums zu machen.
8	Liz ________________ quite a lot of money.	Liz **verdient** ziemlich viel Geld.
9	Tom is ____________________________.	Tom ist **fleißig**.
10	Rish's parents are very ________________.	Rishis Eltern sind sehr **reich**.
11	Jacob is a ________________ artist.	Jacob ist ein **erfolgreicher** Künstler.

5 What are their jobs?

Sieh dir die Bilder an und schreibe die Berufe auf.

1 

____

2 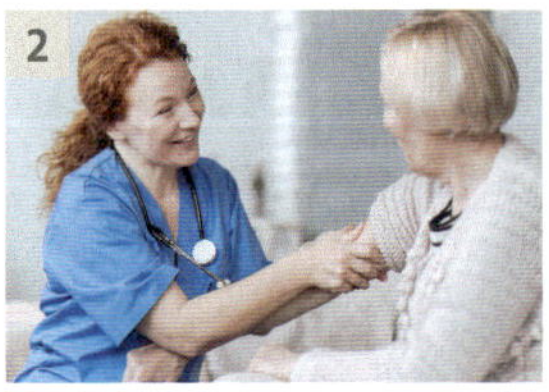

____

3 

____

4 

____

5 

____

6 

____

7 

____

8 

____

▸ Check

6 New words and phrases

▸ SB, pp. 134–135 | VOCABULARY p. 229

1	We ________________ a strange sound in the house but didn't know where it came from.	Wir **bemerkten** ein seltsames Geräusch im Haus, wussten aber nicht, woher es kam.
2	Who ________________________________ in your family?	Wer **wäscht die Wäsche** in deiner Familie?
3	________________ your T-shirts before you put them in the wardrobe.	**Falte** deine T-Shirts, bevor du sie in den Schrank legst.
4	We ________________ our neighbours' cat when they're on holiday.	Wir **kümmern** uns um die Katze unserer Nachbarn, wenn sie im Urlaub sind.
5	________________ the cute dog over there!	**Schau** dir den süßen Hund dort drüben **an**!
6	Let's ________________ a nice present for Tarek.	Lasst uns **nach** einem schönen Geschenk für Tarek **suchen**.
7	"What's *'Sahne'* in English?" – "I don't know. ________ it ________ in a dictionary.	„Was heißt *‚Sahne'* auf Englisch?" – „Ich weiß es nicht. **Schlag** es in einem Wörterbuch **nach**."
8	Sometimes Jim has to ________________ his little brother.	Manchmal muss Jim seinen kleinen Bruder **babysitten**.
9	Molly often ________________ her sister when their parents weren't at home.	Molly hat ihre Schwester oft **gebabysittet**, wenn ihre Eltern nicht zu Hause waren.
10	Phil earns some money with ________________.	Phil verdient etwas Geld mit **Babysitten**.
11	Please ________________ the ________________ when it's finished.	Bitte **leere** die **Geschirrspülmaschine**, wenn sie fertig ist.
12	Some people ________________ the cold.	Manche Menschen **hassen** die Kälte.
13	Taking out the rubbish is my ________________ favourite chore.	Den Müll rausbringen ist die Arbeit, die ich **am wenigsten** gerne mache.
14	It takes ________________ two hours to go from Brighton to London by car.	Es dauert **mindestens** zwei Stunden, um mit dem Auto von Brighton nach London zu fahren.

7 Listen carefully!

10

Höre dir die Sätze aufmerksam an und schreibe das fehlende Wort in die Lücke.

1 Laura, what are your plans for the ____________________?

2 It's not easy to make good ____________________.

3 I think I want to be a ____________________.

4 I won't ____________________ as much as a programmer, but that's OK.

5 My sister is a ____________________ banker.

6 Alfie and Tess want to start a ____________________.

7 What ____________________ do you have to do?

8 I have to empty the ____________________.

8 New words and phrases

▶ SB, p. 136 | VOCABULARY pp. 229–230

1	The Christmas concert was a ______________.	Das Weihnachtskonzert war ein **Hochgenuss**.
2	Do you get ____________________?	Bekommst du **Taschengeld**?
3	Do you read books or ______________?	Liest du Bücher oder **Zeitschriften**?
4	We need to ______________ for food today.	Wir müssen heute Lebensmittel **einkaufen**.
5	There's too much ______________ in my wardrobe. I don't wear most of it any more.	Ich habe zu viel **Zeug** in meinem Schrank. Das meiste davon ziehe ich gar nicht mehr an.
6	Do you want to pay ______________.	Möchten Sie **bar** bezahlen?
7	Can I pay ______________?	Kann ich **mit Karte** bezahlen?
8	Where is the next ____________________?	Wo ist der nächste **Geldautomat**?
9	The ring was a ______________ from my aunt.	Der Ring war ein **Geschenk** meiner Tante.
10	Before we go home, I want to buy a few things at the ____________________.	Bevor wir nach Hause fahren, möchte ich ein paar Dinge im **Souvenirladen** kaufen.
11	I have £250 in my ____________________ ____________________.	Ich habe 250£ auf meinem **Sparkonto**.
12	Mary works in a ______________.	Mary arbeitet in einer **Bank**.
13	Grandma collects ______________.	Großmutter sammelt **Münzen**.
14	I have some money in my ______________ ____________________.	Ich habe etwas Geld in meinem **Sparschwein**.

▶ Check

9 New words and phrases

▸ SB, p. 137 | VOCABULARY pp. 230–231

1	Our ______________ sells delicious cakes.	Unsere **Bäckerei** verkauft leckere Kuchen.
2	______________ need to get up very early.	**Bäcker/innen** müssen sehr früh aufstehen.
3	Let's ______________ a cake together.	Lass uns zusammen einen Kuchen **backen**.
4	Ken works in an ______________ shop.	Ken arbeitet in einem **Elektronik**geschäft.
5	Jane is a ______________.	Jane ist **Zeitungshändlerin**.
6	Lara buys sports magazines at the ______________ near her house.	Lara kauft Sportmagazine im **Zeitschriftenladen** in der Nähe ihres Hauses.

10 New words and phrases

▸ SB, p. 138 | VOCABULARY p. 231

1	What ______________ do you take?	Welche **Größe** haben Sie?
2	This T-shirt is too ______________.	Dieses T-Shirt ist zu **groß**.
3	We can't buy the house. The ______________ is too high.	Wir können das Haus nicht kaufen. Der **Preis** ist zu hoch.
4	Lara is happy. She won a ______________ in the maths competition.	Lara ist glücklich. Sie hat einen **Preis** im Mathe-Wettbewerb gewonnen.
5	______________ the dress?	**Was kostet** das Kleid?
6	______________ the shoes?	**Was kosten** die Schuhe?
7	Here's your ______________.	Hier ist Ihr **Wechselgeld**.
8	These shoes are nice but I like ______________ over there better.	Diese Schuhe sind schön, aber ich mag **die dort** drüben lieber.
9	Can I ______________ this dress, please?	Kann ich bitte dieses Kleid **anprobieren**?

11 New words and phrases

▸ SB, p. 139 | VOCABULARY p. 232

1	Let's ask a ______________ to bring you the dress in your size.	Lass uns eine/n **Verkäufer/in** bitten, dir das Kleid in deiner Größe zu bringen.
2	"How much are the T-shirts?" – "They're £25 ______________."	„Was kosten die T-Shirts?" – „Die kosten **jeweils** 25 Pfund."
3	Sam is our best ______________.	Sam ist unser bester **Kunde**.
4	______________ ______________?	**Möchten Sie sonst noch etwas?**

12 Lost words

Vervollständige die Sätze mit den Wörtern aus den Luftballons.

1 Look _at_ that great bike over there!

2 I'd like to try these trousers ______________.

3 It's hard to make predictions ______________ the weather next month.

4 Do you believe ______________ god?

5 Sue is ______________ the hairdresser's.

6 Tom has to look ______________ his little brother this afternoon.

7 Do you want to pay ______________ cash or ______________ card?

8 We have to shop ______________ clothes next week.

9 Please be quiet and show some respect ______________ the musicians.

10 Excuse me, I'm looking ______________ a pair ______________ walking boots.

13 New words and phrases

▸ SB, pp. 140–141 | VOCABULARY p. 232

1	I want to ______________ my old bike and ______________ a better one.	Ich möchte mein altes Fahrrad **verkaufen** und mir ein besseres **kaufen**.
2	So far we ______________ 100 tickets for the school concert.	Bisher **haben** wir 100 Karten für das Schulkonzert **verkauft**.
3	We'll ______________ Brighton soon.	Wir werden bald **nach** Brighton **ziehen**.
4	My grandparents live far away. I really ______________ them.	Meine Großeltern leben weit entfernt. Ich **vermisse** sie.
5	I wrote my parents a letter and sent them a big ______________.	Ich habe meinen Eltern einen Brief geschrieben und ihnen eine große **Umarmung** geschickt.
6	________ you ______________ your friends when you meet?	**Umarmst** du deine Freunde, wenn ihr euch trefft?
7	Dan and Mia love ______________ and want to get married soon.	Dan und Mia lieben **einander** und wollen bald heiraten.
8	Where do you want to do ______________________________?	Wo möchtest du ein **Praktikum** machen?

▸ Check

14 New words and phrases

▸ SB, p. 142 | VOCABULARY pp. 232–233

1 Please ____________ your name.	Bitte **wiederhole** deinen Namen.
2 Let's stay in ____________!	Lass uns in **Kontakt** bleiben.
3 Olivia's ____________ is her creativity.	Olivias **Stärke** ist ihre Kreativität.
4 Tarek is very ____________ because he does a lot of sport.	Tarek ist sehr **stark**, weil er sehr viel Sport macht.
5 I can't ____________ the puzzle.	Ich kann das Rätsel nicht **lösen**.

15 Listen carefully!

11

Höre dir die Sätze aufmerksam an und schreibe das fehlende Wort in die Lücke.

1 We ____________________ our car last month.

2 We got a good ____________________ for it.

3 There's quite a lot of money in my ____________________.

4 Let's get some fresh bread from the ____________________.

5 There's a ____________________ outside the supermarket.

6 Please ____________________ your family name.

7 One of Alfie's ____________________ is that he is a good listener.

8 Last year he did some ____________________ at a hospital.

16 New words and phrases

▸ SB, p. 144 | VOCABULARY p. 233

1 ____________ Mia, please come to my party.	**Liebe** Mia, bitte komm zu meiner Party.
2 ________________________?	**Wie geht es dir/euch/Ihnen?**
3 Sarah always ________________ the weekend.	Sarah **freut sich** immer **auf** das Wochenende.
4 I ________________________ ____________ from you.	Ich **freue mich darauf**, von dir **zu hören**.
5 ________________________.	**Pass auf dich auf.**
6 Farid ____________ four languages.	Farid **versteht** vier Sprachen.
7 Do you think Paul ____________ what we said?	Glaubst du, Paul **hat verstanden**, was wir gesagt haben?

17 New words and phrases

► SB, p. 145 | VOCABULARY p. 233

1	Do you believe in ________________?	Glaubst du an **Horoskope**?
2	Do you know your ________________?	Kennst du dein **Sternzeichen**?
3	That was ________________ information.	Das waren **nützliche** Informationen.
4	Do you think your plan is ________________?	Glaubst du, dein Plan ist **realistisch**?

18 Picture crossword

Sieh dir die Bilder an und trage die richtigen Wörter in das Gitter ein.

1

2
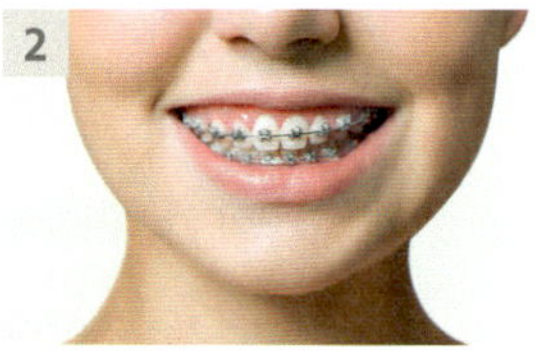

3

4

5

6

7

8

9

10

11

12

13

► Check

19 Let's talk: Über Berufe und die Zukunft sprechen

► SB, p. 198

Ein Freund/eine Freundin, mit dem/der du dich auf Englisch unterhältst, fragt dich nach deinem Berufswunsch, den Berufen deiner Eltern und nach deinen Wünschen für die Zukunft. Erzähle ihm/ihr, was du werden wolltest, als du jünger warst, was du jetzt werden möchtest, welche Berufe deine Eltern haben und wie du dir dein Leben in der Zukunft vorstellst.

Start like this:

When I was little, I ...	My mum is a ...	In the future I'll ...
Now I ...	My dad is a ...	Perhaps I'll ...

20 Let's talk: Einkaufen und über Preise sprechen

► SB, p. 199

Sieh dir die beiden Bilder an und schreibe zwei passende Dialoge dazu. In Bild 1 bittet das Mädchen (B) die Verkäuferin (A) um Hilfe. Sie möchte die Hose in Größe M und das Kleid in Blau. Sie möchte beides anprobieren. In Bild 2 möchte das Mädchen (B) die Kleidung bar bezahlen und bittet die Kassiererin (C) um eine Tragetasche. Sie bekommt Wechselgeld und die Tasche und verabschiedet sich höflich.

A: Can ________________________________?

B: Yes, please. Do you ________________________

________________________________?

A: I'll go and see if we have them in size M. What about the dress?

B: Do you have ________________________?

Shop assistant comes back with trousers and dress.

A: Here you are.

B: Thank you. Can I ________________________?

A: Yes, of course, the changing rooms are over there.

C: How would you like to pay?

B: I'd like ________________________________.

C: OK. That's £ 125.98.

B: I'd ________________________, please.

C: No problem, and here's your

________________________________.

B: ________________________________.

C: Bye.

BASIC
lighthouse 2

Wordmaster

Im Auftrag des Verlages erarbeitet von
Ursula Fleischhauer, Hannover

In Zusammenarbeit mit der Englischredaktion
Klaus Unger (Projektleitung), Lisa Ahmadi sowie
Elizabeth Pancake-Steeg und Chelsea Ledvinka-Heß

Medienmanagement
Silke Kirchhoff

Illustrationen
Evelt Yanait, Advocate Art
Scout-Illustrationen: Irina Zinner, Hamburg

Fotos
Anja Poehlmann, Brighton
Für die freundliche Unterstützung danken wir der
Varndean School, Brighton

Umschlaggestaltung
Rosendahl, Berlin

Layoutkonzept
Klein & Halm, Berlin

Layout und technische Umsetzung
PER MEDIEN & MARKETING GmbH, Braunschweig

Audio-Dateien
Studio
Clarity Studio, Berlin
Regie und Aufnahmeleitung
Susanne Kreutzer
Tontechnik
Dimitris Kritikos

Druck
Athesiadruck GmbH

PEFC-zertifiziert
Dieses Produkt stammt aus nachhaltig bewirtschafteten Wäldern und kontrollierten Quellen
PEFC/18-31-166
www.pefc.de

www.cornelsen.de

1. Auflage, 1. Druck 2024
978-3-06-034632-5

Quellenverzeichnis

Cover
Cornelsen/Personen am Strand: Anja Poehlmann, Strandhäuschen: Shutterstock.com/JoolsW

Illustrationen
Cornelsen/**Evelt Yanait**, Advocate Art: S. 4, S. 7/o.r., S. 11, S. 15/u.r., S. 20, S. 23, S. 26, S. 42/3, S. 42/9, S. 43, S. 49, S. 53, S. 60/o.r., S. 63; Cornelsen/**Irina Zinner**: S. 1, S. 18/u.r., S. 27, S. 42/o.r., S. 48, S. 58/o.r., S. 60/u.r.

Abbildungen
S. 2: Shutterstock.com/Madeleine Forsberg; **S. 3:** Shutterstock.com/Goxy Belgrade; **S. 7/u.r.:** Shutterstock.com/prapass; **S. 8:** stock.adobe.com/Valerii Honcharuk; **S. 9/o.r.:** Shutterstock.com/wavebreakmedia; **S. 9/u.r.:** stock.adobe.com/goir; **S. 12/1:** Shutterstock.com/New Africa; **S. 12/2:** stock.adobe.com/blazic27; **S. 12/3:** stock.adobe.com/Goffkein; **S. 12/4:** stock.adobe.com/Мар'ян Філь; **S. 12/6:** stock.adobe.com/Zuni; **S. 12/7:** stock.adobe.com/Wayhome Studio; **S. 15/o.r.:** Shutterstock.com/LightField Studios; **S. 16/m.r.:** stock.adobe.com/freshidea; **S. 16/o.r.:** Shutterstock.com/In Green; **S. 17:** Shutterstock.com/Eric Isselee; **S. 18/m.r.:** stock.adobe.com/Aisyaqilumar; **S. 19:** stock.adobe.com/Alexandra_K; **S. 22:** Shutterstock.com/rururu1111; **S. 25:** Shutterstock.com/Madeleine Forsberg; **S. 40:** Shutterstock.com/BY213; **S. 42/1:** Shutterstock.com/Ian Francis; **S. 42/10:** Shutterstock.com/yevgeniy11; **S. 42/2:** stock.adobe.com/fotopic; **S. 42/4:** stock.adobe.com/Daniel Prudek; **S. 42/5:** stock.adobe.com/Studio D; **S. 42/6:** stock.adobe.com/Kovac; **S. 42/7:** stock.adobe.com/Tierney; **S. 42/8:** stock.adobe.com/iracosma; **S. 44:** stock.adobe.com/by-studio; **S. 45:** Shutterstock.com/Marti Bug Catcher; **S. 46:** stock.adobe.com/Alproduction; **S. 47:** Shutterstock.com/Ranta Images; **S. 51:** stock.adobe.com/ttonaorh; **S. 52/1:** Shutterstock.com/Moving Moment; **S. 52/10:** stock.adobe.com/Olga Koronyevska; **S. 52/2:** Shutterstock.com/del-Mar; **S. 52/3:** stock.adobe.com; **S. 52/4:** stock.adobe.com/Alexandra_K; **S. 52/5:** Shutterstock.com/Marti Bug Catcher; **S. 52/6:** Shutterstock.com/mexrix; **S. 52/7:** stock.adobe.com/BillionPhotos.com; **S. 52/8:** stock.adobe.com/Lucas; **S. 52/9:** stock.adobe.com/SFIO CRACHO; **S. 54:** Shutterstock.com/Olena Yakobchuk; **S. 56/1:** Shutterstock.com/kurhan; **S. 56/2:** stock.adobe.com/zinkevych; **S. 56/3:** Shutterstock.com/Krakenimages.com; **S. 56/4:** Shutterstock.com/KANGWANS; **S. 56/5:** stock.adobe.com/Rawpixel.com; **S. 56/6:** Shutterstock.com/Elle Aon; **S. 56/7:** stock.adobe.com/DragonImages; **S. 56/8:** stock.adobe.com/nishihata; **S. 57:** Shutterstock.com/Utekhina Anna; **S. 58/u.r.:** stock.adobe.com/Сергей Луговский; **S. 59:** stock.adobe.com/afxhome; **S. 61:** stock.adobe.com/Pineapple studio; **S. 62/1:** stock.adobe.com/conzorb; **S. 62/10:** Shutterstock.com/RossHelen; **S. 62/11:** stock.adobe.com/AkuAku; **S. 62/12:** Shutterstock.com/CarlosDavid; **S. 62/13:** Shutterstock.com/Maxx-Studio; **S. 62/2:** Shutterstock.com/Aleksandr Rybalko; **S. 62/3:** Shutterstock.com/Didecs; **S. 62/4:** Shutterstock.com/New Africa; **S. 62/5:** Shutterstock.com/New Africa; **S. 62/6:** stock.adobe.com/Cozine; **S. 62/7:** stock.adobe.com/Сергей Луговский; **S. 62/8:** stock.adobe.com/Hatia; **S. 62/9:** Shutterstock.com/Hadrian; **S. 62/o.r.:** Shutterstock.com/Net Vector.